THE
SACKETT BRAND

THE
SACKETT BRAND
LOUIS L'AMOUR

BANTAM BOOKS
NEW YORK • TORONTO • LONDON • SYDNEY • AUCKLAND

THE SACKETT BRAND
A Random House Direct, Inc. Book
Published in arrangement with
Bantam Books, Inc.
1540 Broadway
New York, NY 10036

PRINTING HISTORY
A Bantam Book / June 1965
The Louis L'Amour Collection / September 1999

If you want to purchase more of these titles, please write to:
The Louis L'Amour Collection
201 East 50th Street
New York, NY 10022

ISBN: 1-58165-115-5

Published simultaneously in the United States and Canada

PRINTED IN THE UNITED STATES OF AMERICA

To Jud and Red,
At Tucumcari and Santa Rosa,
A Long Time Ago....

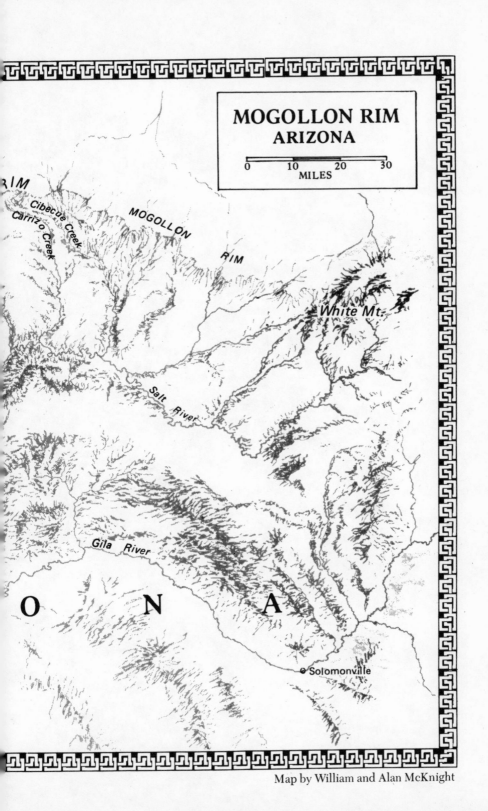

MOGOLLON RIM
ARIZONA

0   10   20   30
MILES

RIM

Cibecue Creek

Carrizo Creek

MOGOLLON

RIM

White Mt.

Salt River

Gila River

O   N   A

Solomonville

Map by William and Alan McKnight

THE
SACKETT BRAND

ONE

Nobody could rightly say any of us Sacketts were what you'd call superstitious. Nonetheless, if I had tied a knot in a towel or left a shovel in the fire nothing might have happened.

The trouble was, when I walked out on that point my mind went a-rambling like wild geese down a western sky.

What I looked upon was a sight of lovely country. Right at my feet was the river, a-churning and a-thrashing at least six hundred feet below me, with here and there a deep blue pool. Across the river, and clean to the horizon to the north and east of me, was the finest stand of pine timber this side of the Smokies.

Knobs of craggy rock thrust up, with occasional ridges showing bare spines to the westward where the timber thinned out and the country finally became desert. In front of me, but miles away, a gigantic wall reared up. That wall was at least a thousand feet higher than where I now stood, though this was high ground.

Down around Globe I'd heard talk of that wall. On the maps I'd seen it was written Mogollon, but folks in the country around called it the Muggy-own.

This was the place we had been seeking, and now I was scouting a route for my wagon and stock. As I stood there on that high point I thought I saw a likely route, and I started to turn away. It was a move I never completed, for something struck me an awful wallop alongside the skull, and next thing I knew I was falling.

Falling? With a six-hundred-foot drop below me? Fear

1

clawed at my throat, and I heard a wild, ugly cry...my own cry.

Then my shoulder smashed into an outcropping of crumbly rock that went to pieces under the impact, and again I was falling; I struck again, fell again, and struck again, this time feet first, facing a gravelly slope that threw me off into the air once more. This time I landed sliding on a sheer rock face that rounded inward and let me fall again, feet first.

Brush growing out from the side of the mountain caught me for just a moment, but I ripped through it, clawing for a grip; then I fell clear into a deep pool.

Down I went, and when I thought to strike out and swim, something snagged my pants leg and started me kicking wildly to shake loose. Then something gave way down there under water, and I shot to the surface right at the spillway of the pool.

My mouth gasped for air, and a wave hit me full in the mouth and almost strangled me, while the force of the water swept me between the rocks and over a six-foot fall. The current rushed me on, and I went through another spillway before I managed to get my feet under me in shallow water.

Even then, stepping on a slippery rock, I fell once more, and this time the current dropped me to a still lower pool, almost covered by arching trees. Flailing with arms and legs, I managed to lay hand to a root and tug myself out of the water. There was a dark hole under the roots of a huge old sycamore that leaned over the water, and it was instinct more than good sense that made me crawl into it before I collapsed.

And then for a long time I felt nothing, heard nothing.

It was the cold that woke me. Shivering, shaking, I struggled back to something like consciousness. At first I sensed only the cold...and then I realized that somebody was talking nearby.

"What's the boss so wrought up about? He was just a driftin' cowpoke."

"You ain't paid to question the boss, Dancer. He said we

were to find him and kill him, and he said we were to hunt for a week if necessary, but he wants the body found and he wants it buried deep. If it ain't dead, we kill it."

"You funnin' me? Why, that poor benighted heathen fell six hundred feet! And you can just bet he was dead before he even started to fall. Macon couldn't miss a shot at that distance, with his target standing still, like that."

"That doesn't matter. We hunt until we find him."

The sound of their walking horses faded out, and I lay still on the wet ground, shaking with chill, knowing I'd got to get warm or die. When I tried to move my arm it flopped out like a dead thing, it was that numb.

My fingers laid hold of a rock that was frozen into the ground and I hauled myself deeper into the hole. The earth beneath me was frozen mud, but it was shelter of a kind, so I curled up like a new-born baby and tried to think.

Who was I? Where was I? Who wanted me dead, and why?

My thoughts were all fuzzy, and I couldn't sort out anything that made sense. My skull throbbed with a dull, heavy beat, and I squinted my eyes against the pain. One leg was so stiff it would scarcely move, and when I got a look at my hands I didn't want to look at them again. When I'd hit the face of the cliff I'd torn nearly all the skin off grabbing for a hold. One fingernail was gone.

Somebody named Macon had shot at me, but so far as I could recall I had never known anybody by that name. But that sudden blow on the head when I started to turn away from the cliff edge must have been it, and that turn had probably saved my life. I put my fingers up and drew them away quickly. There was a raw furrow in my scalp just above the ear.

The cold had awakened me; the voices had started me thinking. The two together had given me a chance to live. Yet why should I try? I had only to lie still and I would die soon enough. All the struggle, all the pain would be over.

And then it struck me.

Ange...Ange Kerry, the girl who had become my wife. Where was *she?*

When I thought of her I rolled over and started to get up. Ange was back up there on the mountain with the wagon and the cattle, and she was alone. She was back there waiting for me, worrying. *And she was alone.*

It was growing dark, and whatever search for me was being carried on would end with darkness, for that day, at least. If I was to make a move, I had to start now.

Using my elbow and hand, I worked my way out of the hole and pulled myself up by clinging to the sycamore. At the same time I kept my body close to it for concealment.

The forest along the stream was open, almost empty of underbrush, but the huge old sycamores made almost a solid roof overhead, so that where I stood it was already twilight.

My teeth rattled with cold, for my shirt was torn to shreds, my pants torn, my boots gone. My gun belt had been ripped loose in the fall and my gun was gone, and with it my bowie knife.

There was no snow, but the cold was icy. Pounding my arm against my body, I tried to get the blood to flowing, to get some warmth into me. One leg I simply could not use, but from the feel of it I was sure it was not broken.

Shelter...I must find shelter and warmth. If I could get to the wagon, I could get clothing, blankets, and a gun. Most of all, I could see Ange, could be sure she was all right.

But first I must think. Only by thought had man prevailed, or so I'd heard somewhere. Panic was the enemy now, more to be feared than the cold, or even that nameless enemy who had struck at me, and now was searching for me with many men.

Who could it be? And why?

This was wild country—actually it was Apache country, and there were few white men around, and nobody who knew me.

So far as I knew, nobody was even aware that we were

in this part of the country.... Yes, there was somebody—the storekeeper in Globe of whom we'd made inquiries. No doubt others had seen us around Globe, but I had no enemies there, nor had I talked to anyone else, nor done anything to offend anyone.

Now, step by careful step, I eased away from the river and into the deeper forest. The sun was setting, and gave me my direction.

Movement awakened pain. A million tiny prickles came into my numbed leg, but I kept on, as careful as I could be under the conditions, wanting to leave no trail that could be followed.

As I crawled up a bank, my hand closed over a rounded rock with an edge. It was a crude, prehistoric hand-axe.

I remembered that Leo Prager, a Boston college man who had spent some time on Tyrel's ranch near Mora, had told me about such things. He had spent all his time hunting for signs of the ancient people who lived in that country before the Indians came—or at any rate, the kind of Indians we knew.

For several weeks I'd guided him around, camped with him, and helped him look, so naturally I learned a good bit about those long-ago people and their ways. When it came to chipping arrowheads, I was the one who could show him how it was done, for I'd grown up around Cherokee boys back in the Tennessee mountains.

What I had found just now was an oval stone about as big as my fist, chipped to an edge along one side, so I had me a weapon. Clinging to it, I crawled over the bank and got to my feet.

I could not be sure how far downstream the river had carried me, but it was likely no more than half a mile. And I knew that after I left Ange and my outfit I had ridden five or six miles before reaching that point where I'd been shot.

So I made a start. Under ordinary conditions I might have walked the distance in two to three hours, but the conditions were not exactly ordinary. I was in bad shape, with a game leg and more hurts than I cared to think on. And with every step I had to be wary of discovery. Moreover, it was rough country, over rocks and through trees and brush, and I'd have to climb some to make up the ground I'd lost in the fall.

How many times I fell down I'll never know, or how many times I crawled on the ground or pulled myself up by a tree or rock. Yet each time I did get up, and somehow I kept pushing along. Finally, unable to go any further, I found a shallow, wind-hollowed cave almost concealed behind a bush, a cave scarcely large enough to take my body, and I crawled in, and there I slept.

Hours later, awakened by the cold, I turned over and worked myself in a little further, and then I slept again. When at last the long, miserable night was past, I awoke in the gray-yellow dawn to face the stark realization that I was a hunted man.

My feet, which had been torn and lacerated by the fall and the night's walking over rocks and frozen ground, seemed themselves almost frozen. My socks were gone, and probably the shreds of them marked my trail.

Numb and cold as I was, I fought to corral my thoughts and point them toward a solution. I knew that what lay before me was no easy thing.

By now Ange would know that I was in serious trouble, for I'd never spent the night away from her side; and it could be that my horse had returned to the wagon. My riderless horse could only mean something awfully wrong.

From the trunk of a big old sycamore, I hacked out two rectangles of bark. Then with rawhide strips cut from my belt with my stone axe and my teeth, I tied those pieces of bark under my feet to protect the soles.

Next, I dug into the ground with the hand-axe and worked until I found a long, limber root, to make a loop large enough to go over my head. Then I broke evergreen boughs from the trees and hung them by their forks or tied them to the loop, making myself a sort of a cape of boughs. It wasn't much, but it cut the force of the wind and kept some of the warmth of my body close to me.

With more time, I could have done better, but I felt I hadn't time to spare. My right leg was badly swollen, but nothing could be done for it now. By the time I finished my crude cape my hands were bleeding. Using a dead branch for a staff, I started off, keeping under cover as best I could.

If I had covered one mile the night before, I was lucky, and there were several miles to go. But I was sure that at first they would be hunting a body along the river—until they found some sign.

By the time the sun was high I was working my way up a canyon where cypresses grew. On my right was the wall of Buckhead Mesa, and I'd left Ange and the wagon on the north side of that mesa. I thought of the rifle and the spare pistol in that wagon…if I could get to it.

Then, far behind me, I heard a loud halloo. That stopped me, and I stood for a moment, catching my breath and listening. It must be that somebody had found some sign, and had called the others. At least, I had to read it that way. From now on, they would know they were hunting a living man.

If they knew of the wagon—and I had to take it they did—they had little to worry about. How many were hunting me I had no idea, but they had only to string out and make a sweep of the country, pushing in toward the wall of the mesa. Using the river as a base line, they could sweep the country, and then climb the mesa and move in on the wagon. It left me very little chance for escape.

My mind shied from thinking of my condition after that fall. I knew I was in bad shape, but I was scared to know how bad, because until I reached Ange and the wagon there was just nothing I could do about it. Right then I wanted a gun in my hand more than I wanted medicine or even a doctor. I wanted a gun and a chance at the man who had ambushed me.

Using the stick, I could sort of hitch along in spite of my bad leg. It didn't seem to be broken, but it had swollen until the pants seam was likely to bust; if it kept on swelling I'd have to split the seam somehow. My hands were in awful shape, and the cut on my skull was a nasty one. I had a stitch in my side, as if maybe I had cracked some ribs. But I wasn't complaining—by rights I should have been dead.

When I was shot I had been standing on a point on Black Mesa, which tied to Buckhead Mesa on the southeast. The canyon where the cypress grew seemed to reach back toward the west side of Buckhead, and from where I was now standing it seemed to offer a chance to follow it back up to the top of Buckhead. So I started out.

You never saw so much brush, so many trees, so many rock falls crammed into one canyon. Fire had swept along the canyon a time or two, leaving some charred logs, but the trees had had time to grow tall again, and the brush had grown thicker than ever, as it always does after a fire.

One thing I had in my favor. Nobody was likely to try taking a horse up that canyon, and if I knew cowpunchers they weren't going to get down from the saddle and scramble on foot up the canyon unless all hell was a-driving them.

A cowhand is a damned fool who will work twenty-five hours out of every day if he can do it from a saddle. But put him on his feet, and you've got yourself a man who is likely to sit down and build himself a smoke so's he can think about it. And after he thinks it over, he'll get back in the saddle and ride off.

It was still cold...bitter cold. I tried not to think of that, but just kept inching along. Sometimes I pulled myself along by grasping branches or clutching at cracks in the rock. Cold as it was, I started to sweat, and that scared me. If that sweat froze, the heat in my body would be used up fighting its cold and I'd die.

Once I broke a hole in the ice and drank, but most of the time I just kept moving because I'd never learned how to quit. I was just a big raw-boned cowboy with big shoulders and big hands who was never much account except for hard work and fighting. Back in the Tennessee hills they used to say my feet were too big for dancing and I hadn't any ear for music; but along about fighting time I'd be there—fist, gun, or bowie knife. All of us Sacketts were pretty much on the shoot.

By noontime I was breasting the rise at the head of the canyon. Only a few yards away the rock of the mesa broke off sharply and dipped into another canyon, while the great flat surface of Buckhead lay on my right. It was several miles in area and thickly forested.

Crawling back into the brush, I settled down to rest a bit and to try thinking things out. My head wasn't working too well and my thoughts came slow, and everything looked different somehow. I kept passing my hand over my forehead and scowling, trying to rid my eyes of the blur.

Near as I could figure, Ange and the wagon were now about three miles off, and moving as I had to, it might take me to sundown to cover that distance. Long before that, every inch of the mesa top would be scoured by riders who would seek out every clump of brush, every tree, every hole in the rocks.

Nobody ever denied that I was a tough man. I stand six feet three in my socks, when I own a pair, and I weigh a hundred and eighty, most of it in my shoulders and arms. I ain't what you'd call a pretty-built man, but when I take hold things generally move.

But now I was weak as a sick cat. I'd lost a sight of blood, and used myself almighty bad. The way things stood, I couldn't run and I couldn't fight. If they found me they had me, and no two ways about it...and they were hunting to kill.

There was no way across that mesa but to walk or crawl, and there was no place a rider couldn't go. It looked to me as if I needed more of a weapon than that hand-axe I had in my pocket.

Turning around, I crawled deeper into the brush and

burrowed down into the pine needles. My head ached, my eyes blinked slowly. I was tired, almighty tired. I felt wore out.

Ange, Ange girl, I said, *I just ain't a-gonna make it. I ain't a-gonna make it right now.*

I was trying to burrow deeper, and then I stopped all movement when I heard a horse walking on frozen ground, but the sound faded off in the distance.

My head felt all swelled up like a balloon, and I couldn't seem to lift it off the ground.

Ange, I said, *damn it, Ange, I...*

TWO

Leaning my shoulder against the rough bark of a tree, I stared at the empty clearing, unwilling to believe what my eyes saw.

The wagon was gone!

Under the wide white moon the clearing lay etched in stillness. The surrounding trees were a wall of blackness against which nothing moved. Within the clearing itself, scarcely two acres in extent, there was nothing.

To this place I had come after hours of unconsciousness or sleep, after hours of fitful struggle for some kind of comfort on the frozen ground, in the numbing cold.

Only when darkness had come had I dared move, for riders had been all about me, searching relentlessly. Once, off to the right I heard faint voices, glimpsed the flicker of a fire.

How many times they might have passed nearby I had no idea, for only occasionally was I even fully aware of things around me. Yet with the deepening shadows some inner alarm had shaken me awake, and after a moment of listening, I rolled from the pine needles in which I had buried myself, and taking up my stick, I pushed myself to my feet.

All through my pain-racked day I had longed for this place and dreamed of arriving here. In the wagon there would be things to help me, in the wagon there would be weapons. Above all, Ange would be there, and I could be sure she was all right.

But she was gone.

Now, more even than care for my wounds I wanted weapons. Above all, I was a fighting man ... it was deeply ingrained

11

in my being, a part of me. Hurt, I would fight; dying, I would still try to fight.

A quiet man I was, and not one to provoke a quarrel, but if set upon I would fight back. I do not say this in boasting, for it was as much a part of me as the beating of my heart. It was bred in the blood-line of those from whom I come, and I could not be other than I am.

This it was, and my love for Ange, that had carried me here. Ange, who had brought love and tenderness to the big, homely man that I am.

Ange knew me well, and she knew I was not a man to die easily. She knew the wild lands herself, and she would have believed that she had only to wait and I would return. She would not willingly have left this place without me, knowing that even if I suffered an accident I would somehow return.

And now a curious fact became evident to me. This place, to which I would be sure to come back, was not watched. None of the searching men were here in this most obvious of places. Why?

The simplest reason was that they did not know of it, though a wagon is not an easy thing to conceal, nor are the mules by which it was drawn, nor the cattle. But now they were not here.

Hesitating no longer, and using my staff, I limped into the clearing and stopped where the wagon had stood.

There were no tracks.

I looked to where the fire had been, and there were no coals, no ashes. The stump that I had dragged up for a backlog, which should have been smoldering yet, was gone.

Had I then come to the wrong place? No...the great, lightning-struck pine from the base of which I had gathered dead branches and bark to kindle our fire stood where it had been. The rock where I had sat while cleaning my rifle was there.

But the wagon was gone, the mules, the cattle...and Ange.

Ange, whom I loved. Ange, who was my life; Ange, whom I had found in the high mountains of Colorado and brought home to the ranch of my brother, in Mora.*

The numbness seemed to creep into my brain, the cold held me still. Leaning on my crude staff, hurting in every muscle and ligament, I looked all around me for a clue, and I found none.

I knew she would not have left without me, and if someone or something had forced her to leave, there should still have been tracks.

Horror crept over me. I could feel its ghostly hand crawling on my spine and neck muscles. Some awful thing had happened here, some terrible, frightful thing. The ruthless pursuit of me, the wiping out of tracks here, all of it spoke of a crime; only I refused to allow myself to think of what the crime might be.

Stiffly, I began to move. I would find the camp of those men and see if Ange was there; in any case, I would see who my enemies were. The wagon and the stock must surely be there.

Turning, I started with a lunge, only to have the end of my staff slip on the icy ground. I fell heavily, barely stifling a scream. My hands fought for a grip on the frozen ground and I struggled to get up, and then I must somehow have slipped over on my face and lost consciousness, for when I awoke the sun was shining.

For a time I lay there, letting the sun soak away the chill in my bones, but only half aware of my surroundings. Slowly realization came to me: I was a hunted man, and here I lay almost in the open, at the foot of a pine tree.

Carefully, I started to turn my head. A wave of sickness swept over me, but I persisted.

My eyes came to a focus. There was no sound but the wind in the pines. The clearing was there before me, and it was empty.

*Sackett, Bantam Books.

My mind was alert now, and in the broad daylight I carefully skirted the clearing. There were no tracks anywhere, none to show our arrival, none to show how the wagon had left. It had simply vanished.

I was without weapons, without food, without clothing or shelter, but all I could think of was Ange. Somebody had been so desperate to have her disappear that every evidence of our presence there had been wiped out.

An hour later, I was at the clearing where their camp had been the night before, but now all were gone. At least a dozen men had slept there, and there were tracks in profusion. Cigarette butts were scattered about, a coffeepot had been emptied, and a crust of bread lay upon the ground.

But there were no wagon tracks, no tracks of small boots for which I searched. And knowing Ange, I knew that she would somehow have contrived to leave a track. She knew me, knew my methods, knew my thoroughness when on trail...and yet, there was nothing. Wherever she was, Ange had never been in this camp.

How could a wagon loaded with more than a ton of supplies, drawn by six big Missouri mules, disappear from a mesa that offered only two or three possible ways by which a wagon might leave it?

Somehow my impression was growing that these men knew nothing of Ange or the wagon. So what then? What had happened? Where was Ange? And who had shot me, and why?

And with these questions there were the others: Why were these men hunting me to kill me? Had they gone for good? Or would they be back?

My hunch was that the search had only begun. Such a desperate search would not be ended that quickly.

I moved off through the trees, hobbling painfully, crawling over fallen logs, occasionally pausing to rest.

When I had left the wagon to scout for a route off Buckhead Mesa, a route into the Tonto Basin, I had skirted the mesa itself and had seen a deep canyon leading off to the southwest. It was all of five hundred feet deep, and it appeared to be wild and impassable, but there was a creek along the bottom. There would be water there, there would be game, there would be fish.

I could no longer look to the wagon for relief. From now on I was completely on my own, alone and without any possible help. And I was surrounded by enemies unknown to me.

By nightfall of a bitterly long day I had found a cave under a natural bridge. The bridge was a tremendous arch of travertine at least a hundred and eighty feet above the waters of the creek, and the cave was a place where a man might hide and where no trouble would come to him unless from some wandering bear or mountain lion. It was a place hidden by brush and the rock slabs all about, a place littered with dead trees brought down by flash floods.

Using the bow and drill method, I started a small fire, and felt warmth working into my muscles. The warmth of the sun had brought some relief from the chill, but not very much.

Making a basin by bending together the corners of a sheet of bark, I heated some water and carefully bathed my hands, then lowered my pants and looked at my leg. It was almost black from bruising, and it was swollen to half again its natural size. For perhaps an hour I sat there, soaking my wounds with a washcloth made from the remnants of my shirt. Whether it would help I did not know, but it felt good.

Then after carefully extinguishing my tiny fire, I put together a bed of evergreen boughs and crawled onto it. I fell into a fitful, troubled sleep.

Hunger woke me from a night of tormented dreams, but first of all I heated water and bathed my leg again, and drank warm water to heat my chilled body. It began to seem as if I would never be warm again, and though I was hungry, what I longed for most was clothing—warm, soft, wonderful clothing.

Sitting there, applying hot cloths to my wounds, I got to thinking on the reason for that attack on me.

As a general run, motives weren't hard to understand there on the frontier. Things were pretty cut and dried, and a body knew where he stood with folks. He knew what his problems were, and the problems of those about him were about the same. A man was too busy trying to stay alive and make some gain, to have time to think much about himself or get his feelings hurt. It seems to me that as soon as a man gets settled down, with meat hung out to smoke and flour in the bin, he starts looking for something to fuss about.

Well, it wasn't that way on the frontier. A man could be just as mean as he was big enough to be; but if he started out to be bad he'd better be big enough or tough enough, if he figured to last. Such folks were usually given time to reach for a gun or they were tucked into a handy noose. I've noticed that the less a man has to worry about getting a living, the more time he has to worry about himself.

Folks on the frontier hadn't any secret sins. The ones who were the kind for such things stayed close to well populated places where they could hide what they were. On the frontier the country was too wide, there was too much open space for a body to be able to cover anything up.

But now somebody wanted me dead, and it was apparently that same somebody who had taken my wagon away, and Ange with it.

I could understand a man wanting a wagon, or a man wanting Ange, and it wasn't ungallant of me to think it was more likely to be the wagon and outfit than Ange. And there was reason for that.

One thing a man didn't do on the frontier was molest a woman, even an all-out bad woman. Women were scarce, and were valued accordingly. Even some pretty mean outlaws had been known to kill a man for jostling a woman on the street.

Pretty soon my leg was feeling better. It was easier to handle, and some of the swelling was gone.

Toward noontime I found me a rabbit. I twisted him out

of a hole with a forked stick, broiled him, and ate him. But a man can't live on rabbits. He needs fat meat.

Several times I saw deer, and once a fat, healthy elk, a big one that would dress two hundred and fifty pounds at least. But what I hunted was something smaller. I couldn't use that much meat, and anyway, I had nothing with which to make a kill.

The afternoon was almost gone and weariness was coming over me when I fetched up at a rocky ledge below a point of Buckhead Mesa. Pine Creek and its wild canyon lay north and west of me, the mesa at my back.

Night was a-coming on, and I wished myself back at my cave. Just as I was fixing to turn back, I smelled smoke. Rather, it was the smell of charred timber, a smell that lingers for days, sometimes for weeks after a burning. That smell can be brought alive again by dampness or rainfall. I knew that somebody had had a fire, and close by.

The ledge was behind some trees and close against the face of the cliff. At this point the cliff was not sheer, though it was very steep, and ended in a mass of rubble, fallen trees, brush, and roots.

I started working my way through the trees. The smell of charred wood grew stronger, and with it the smell of burned flesh.

For the first time I felt real fear, fear for Ange. And with the fear, came certainty. I was sure that when I found that fire, when I found that charred wood and burned flesh, I would find my wagon, and I would find Ange.

THREE

The wire-like brush was thick, and there was no getting through it in my present condition, half naked as I was, without ripping my hide to shreds. What I had to do was seek out a way around and through, and finally I made it. My heart was pounding with slow, heavy beats when at last I came in sight of the burned-out fire.

I had found my wagon, and I had found my mules. But there was no sign of Ange.

The wagon and all that was in it had been burned. The mules, I discovered, had each been shot in the head, then dumped over the cliff one by one. Afterward, somebody had come around and piled brush over the lot, then set fire to it. The killing of those fine big mules hurt me...there'd been no better mules west of Missouri, if anywhere.

A fine gray ash had been left by the burning of desert brush. And it was obvious that anything that scattered when the wagon struck bottom had been carefully picked up and thrown on the heap.

Whoever had done this had made a try at wiping out all sign, just as no tracks had been left on the mesa top. Suddenly it occurred to me that whoever had done this might well come back to make sure the destruction had been complete. If they returned and found me, I would be killed, for I was in no shape to defend myself, nor had I any weapon.

For several minutes I stood there, trying to think it out, and studying that heap of charred wood and burned mules, trying to figure out who could have done this, and why.

The destruction was not total, for all the work somebody

put to make it so, and in thinking about it I could see why. This had been a hurried job.

Careful to disturb things as little as I might, I worked my way around the fire. A big wagon like that, made of white oak, doesn't burn so easy, in spite of the dryness of the wood. The hubs of the wheels were solid, the wagon bed was strongly made....And then I thought of our secret place.

It was a box hollowed out of a block of six-by-six timber and bolted to the underside of the wagon, and in it we kept a few odds and ends of keepsakes and five gold eagles for emergency money. By lifting a wooden pin inside the wagon-box a section of the bottom lifted out. It made a lid for the box.

The canvas top of the wagon and the bows were gone, of course; the wheels were badly charred but almost intact, the body of the wagon was largely destroyed. Poking around in the mess that remained, I found the box, charred, but still whole. Breaking it open, I found the gold money, but what-ever else had been inside was charred to ashes.

Poking around where the grub box had been, I found a can of beans that had tumbled from the box when it busted open, and had rolled down among the rocks. And there was also a charred and partly burned side of bacon. What I had hoped to find was some kind of a weapon—a kitchen knife or anything—but whatever there was must have been buried in the rubble.

There was no telling when the ones who had done this might come back, for they had been bound and determined to destroy all sign of me and my outfit, and I was feeling convinced they would return to make sure the job had been done. I'd been taking care all the time to leave no tracks; now I took a last look around.

There lay the ashes not only of my outfit, but of my hopes as well. Ange and me had planned to start a ranch in the Tonto Basin, and I'd spent most of what I had on that outfit and on the cattle to follow.

It was plain to see from the ways things had been piled

up that somebody had stood here, carefully putting into the pile everything that was scattered, and it made no sense. In this wild country, who would ever know about what had happened here? Many a man had been murdered and just left for the buzzards, and nobody was the wiser. No, whoever and whatever, they not only wanted me dead, but everything wiped out to leave no slightest trace.

So what did that spell for Ange?

Always she was there in my thoughts, but I kept shoving those thoughts of her to the back of my mind. There was nothing I could do to help her, or even to find her, until I could get a weapon and a horse. To think of her was to be frightened, to let myself waste time in worrying—time that I'd best spend doing something. One thing I'd learned over the years: never to waste time moaning about what couldn't be helped. If a body can do something, fine—he should do it. If he can't, then there's no use fussing about it until he *can* do something.

The day was almost gone. Every move I made was hurting me, and I had to move almighty slow. I wanted to get back to that cave under the stone bridge, but before I'd gone a dozen yards I realized I just didn't have it in me. Like it or not, I was going to have to find somewhere close by, and go without a fire.

The ground was hard and my foot slipped on an icy rock, and I went down. The fall shook me up. It took me a minute or two to get up again. I realized that the cold was growing worse. The river, which had been open water when I'd taken my fall off that lookout point, would be frozen over by now.

Finally, when I was only a hundred yards or so from the ruins of my outfit, I found a place where some slabs of rock had tumbled off the mesa's edge, high above, and in falling had formed a low cave, not over five feet deep and just about large enough for me to curl up inside. There was dead brown grass near the cave, so I tugged on it and pulled enough for ground cover, and I crawled in. And then I just passed out.

In the night, I awakened. My first thought was that of

course I knew the names of two of my pursuers. The man who shot me had been called Macon, and then there was Dance, or Dancer. That name had been put to one of the men I'd overheard talking.

I was lying there shivering, when I heard them come back. Only it was not several men, it was only one. The horse came walking along, passing within a few yards of where I lay...I could hear the creak of the saddle, and a faint jingle of spurs.

I was too cold and stiff to move, too badly hurt to be of any use to myself. I heard him rousting around in the dark, and once I heard him swear. Then there was a faint glow, and I thought I could detect the crackle of flames. Some little time went by, and finally I must have dozed off again, because when my eyes opened it was daylight.

For a while I just lay still, and then I half-crawled half-rolled out of my hideaway and, using my staff, pushed myself to my feet. It was not until then that I remembered the rider in the nighttime.

Going down to the dim trail, I found his horse's tracks, coming and going. They were sharp, well-defined tracks, made by a horse whose shoes were in good shape. I studied those tracks for a while, and I was not likely to forget them. Then I went back to the wagon.

I saw that he had piled on more brush and lighted it again. Everything was gone now except those black gum hubs for the wheels. They burn mighty hard, and these had only charred over. The fire still smoldered, so I stayed there a few minutes, warming myself.

I didn't need anybody to tell me that I was in bad shape. Somehow I had to get out of that country and get to where I could be cared for, and where I could get a horse and some guns. And then I recalled talk I'd heard of Camp Verde.

Judging by what I'd heard, it could be not much more than thirty miles or so as a crow would fly; but to get there by covering no more than thirty miles a body would surely have to have wings, just like the crow.

None of us Sacketts ever came equipped with wings, and weren't likely to acquire any, judging by the way we lived or the company we kept. The least likely was me, William Tell Sackett, born in the high Cumberland country of Tennessee.

One thing I did know. I wasn't likely to get to Camp Verde by sitting here thinking about it. So I heated that can of beans over what was left of my own wagon's fire, and split the can open with my stone axe. Then I made shift to eat that whole can. After that I took out, walking.

Starved, half-frozen, and sick from the fever of my wounds and lost blood, I made a start. Pa taught us boys there was never to be any quit in us. "You just get goin' an' *try!*" That was what he used to say, and that was all I could do. Somehow or other I had to keep myself alive and cover the forty or more miles it would be to Camp Verde, over the roughest kind of country. I was going as direct as a body could, for I knew the direction, and I didn't have a horse to hunt trails for.

Somehow I got out of Buckhead Canyon, and then I made myself another pair of bark moccasins—I'd already worn through two pair—and crossed over the ridge.

From the top I could see a dim trail going up the hogback leading to the mesa northwest of Buckhead, and that was my direction. It must have been almost a thousand feet from the top of the ridge to the bottom of Pine Canyon, and I did most of it sitting down, sliding or hitching my way along with my hands and one good leg.

The sun was in mid-sky by the time I got down to the bottom of the canyon. And then by crawling up the other ridge I found that trail.

My hands were bleeding again, and I was lightheaded. One side of my brain recognized that fact, just as if it was standing off to one side watching the whole show. But I kept on going, because I hadn't sense enough to lie down and die.

This was an Indian trail, and in this country that meant Apaches, and I knew a good bit about them. Not as much as my brother Tyrel, but I knew a-plenty. I knew if they found me I might as well throw in my hand.

The Apache was a fighting man. He was a warrior, and that was his pride. His reputation was based on how many horses he could steal and how many coups he could count. By the white man's standards this was all wrong, but the Indian had a different way of looking at it. Mercy to your enemy would be evidence of weakness and fear, and the Indian respected only bravery.

He himself had courage, and he had his own viewpoint of honor. I had respect for the Indians. I'd swapped horses with them, fought with them, hunted with them...but the last thing I wanted to see now was an Indian.

On top of the mesa, I drank deep and long at Clover Spring, and then I set out again. Time and again I fell down, and each time it was harder to get up, yet each time, somehow, I managed it. Camp Verde, I knew, was off there to the northwest, and it was on the Verde River, or close to it. The only thing I had in mind was to get to the East Verde River—the same one that saved my neck when I fell—and follow it along to the Verde, then follow that north to the Camp.

All my sense of time was gone. Several times I heard myself talking, and once or twice even singing. My feet didn't seem to work the way they should, and walking seemed to mean stumbling and falling and getting up again.

And then all of a sudden I was no longer alone. There was an Apache riding on either side of me.

They rode on past and two more came up. They slowed down, walking their horses. They were lithe, bronzed men, dusty from travel, and some of them carried fresh scalps. They did not speak, they did not make any move toward me, they simply watched me out of their flat black eyes. When I fell down they watched me get up. One Apache laughed when I fell and tried to get up, but that was all.

A mile went behind us. I don't know how many times I fell in that mile, maybe nine or ten times. Each time they waited and let me get up, and I just kept on a-going. The trail finally left the mesa for the East Verde, and the Apaches stayed with me.

When the trail reached the end of Polles Mesa they turned, and one of them rode a horse across in front of me. When I tried to go around him, he backed the horse in front of me again and, sick as I was, delirious as I was, I understood I was a prisoner. One of them pointed with a lance, and I turned north up the gorge.

After maybe a mile we came to a rancheria. All the Apaches came out, women and children, staring at me. I saw them standing there, and then I took another step and my knee just bent over and threw me on my face.

Something in my mind was for an instant clear and sharp, and something said, "Tell, you're through. They will kill you."

And then I passed out. I just faded into a black, pain-filled world that softened around the edges until there was no pain, nothing.

FOUR

My eyes had been open for some time before my thoughts fell into place and realization came to me. Over my head was some sort of a brush shelter and I was lying on a couple of deerskins.

Turning my head, I looked down the gentle slope and saw the Apaches. There were six or seven men and twice that many women gathered around a small fire, eating and talking.

It all came back to me then, the Apaches moving up on either side of me, the falling down, the getting up. How long, I wondered, had they followed me?

One of the squaws said something, and a squat, powerfully built Indian got to his feet. He came up the slope, wearing only a headband, breechclout, and the knee-high moccasins favored by the Apache.

He squatted beside me, gesturing toward my leg, the wound on my skull, and my other injuries. And he made the sign for brave man, holding the left fist in front of the body and striking down past it with the right.

"Friend," I said, "*amigo.*"

He touched the bullet scar on my skull. "Apache?"

"White-eye," I replied, using the term they gave to the white man. And I added, "I will find him."

He nodded, and then said, "You hungry?"

"Yes," I said, and after a moment asked, "How long have I been here?"

He held up three fingers, and added, "We go now."

"To Camp Verde?"

For a minute there I thought he was going to smile. There was a kind of grim humor in his eyes as he shook his

25

head. "No Camp Verde." He waved his hand toward the Mogollons. He studied me carefully. "Soldier at Camp Verde."

He paused while I lay there wondering what was going to happen to me. Would they take me along as a prisoner? Or let me go?

"I need guns," I said, "and a horse. I can get them at Verde."

"You very bad," he said. "You all right now?"

Now that there was a question. To tell the truth, I felt as weak as a cat, but I wasn't telling him that, so I told him I was all right. He stood up suddenly and dropped a buckskin sack beside me and then walked away. What would come now I didn't know, and I was too weak to care. So I closed my eyes for a moment and must have passed right out, because when I opened them again it was cold and dark, and there was no smell of fire, no sound or movement.

Crawling from the deerskin bed where I had been lying, I looked all around. I was alone.

They had cared for me, left me, and gone on about their business. I remembered something Cap Rountree had told me once up in Colorado—that there was no accounting for Indians. Most times, finding a white man alone and helpless as I was, they would have killed him without hesitation, unless he was worth torturing first. It was a good chance that they had followed my trail for miles before they caught up, and they were curious about me. There's nothing an Indian respects more than endurance and courage, and to them that was what I was showing on that trail.

Then I thought of the buckskin sack, and I opened it. My hand, and then a taste, told me it was pinole, so I ate a handful of it and hobbled to the spring to wash it down. When I had eaten another handful or two, I crawled back in my lean-to and went to sleep. When I woke I was ready to go on.

Weak I might be, but I was better off than I had been, and on the fourth day after leaving the Apache rancheria, I made Camp Verde. That day I was on the last of my pinole.

The camp was on the mesa some distance back from the river, and the valley right there was six to seven miles wide. They had a few acres of vegetable garden cultivated, and the place looked almighty good. There was a company of cavalry there, two companies of the Eighth Infantry, and forty Indian scouts under a man named Al Seiber, a powerfully muscled scout who was as much Indian as white man in his thinking.

Well, I was in bad shape, but I made out to walk straight coming up to those soldiers. After all, I'd served through the War Between the States myself, and I didn't figure to shame my service.

Folks came out of tents and stores to look at me as I came in, and I must have looked a sight. I'd thrown away my pine-branch coat, and was wearing those deerskins around my shoulders. What I'd left of my pants wouldn't do to keep a ten-year-old boy from shame.

As I came up, there was a man wearing captain's insignia coming out of the trading post. He was walking with a bull-shouldered man in a buckskin shirt. When the captain saw me he pulled up short.

"Captain," I began, "I—"

"Mr. Seiber," the captain interrupted, and he turned to the man by his side, "see that this man is fed, then bring him to my quarters." After a second glance, he added, "You might find him a shirt and a pair of pants, too."

All of a sudden I felt faint. I half fell against the corner of the building and stayed there a moment. I was like that when a sergeant came out of the store, and I never saw a man look more surprised. *"Tell Sackett! I'll be damned!"*

"Hello, Riley," I said, and then I straightened up and followed off after Al Seiber.

Behind me I heard the captain speak. "Sergeant, do you know that man?"

"Yes, sir. He was in the Sixth Cavalry during the war, and he was a sergeant there at the end, acting in command through several engagements. A sharpshooter, sir, and as fine a horseman as you will be likely to find."

Seiber made me sit down, and he poured a tin cup half full of whiskey. "Drink this, man. You need it."

He rustled around, finding some grub and clothes for me. "Apaches?" he asked.

"White men," I said, and then added, "The only Apaches I saw treated me decent."

"They found you?"

So I told him about it as I ate the food he dished up, and he had me describe the Indian.

"You must be shot with luck," he said. "That sounds like Victorio. He's a coming man among them."

Captain Porter was waiting for me when I walked in, and he waved me to a chair. Beat as I was from the days of travel, my hands just beginning to heal, my head in bad shape, I was still too keyed-up for sleep. The Apaches had treated my wounds, how and with what I had no idea.

Taking as little time as I could, I told him about Ange, the unexpected shot, the burned wagon, and the mules.

"If I can buy a horse," I said, "and maybe a pack mule, I'd like to get myself some guns and go back."

"You must feel that way, I suppose," he said, "but your wife must have been killed...murdered, if you will. I understand how you feel; nevertheless, if there are several men against you, as you seem to believe, I am afraid you'll have no success."

He paused. "And that brings me to my problem. I need men. All units here are in need of recruits, and I am allowed six officers. We have only four."

"I was never an officer."

"But you acted in command...for how long?"

"It was two or three times. Maybe four or five months in all."

"And the Sixth Cavalry participated in fifty-seven actions during the war, am I right? You must have been in command during some of those actions."

"Yes, sir."

"I could use you, Mr. Sackett. In fact, I need experienced

men very badly, particularly those who have done some Indian fighting. You have, I presume?"

"Yes, sir. But I have to go back to the Tonto. My wife is back there, Captain."

We talked for almost an hour, and by then I was beginning to feel everything that had happened to me. The three days in the Apache *rancheria* had helped to bring me out of it, but sitting there listening to the captain talking of old wars and far-off places, I suddenly knew I was a long way from being ready for a fight. And yet there could be no delay. Even now Ange might be somewhere needing help, needing me.

"Are there any new outfits in the country?" I asked him abruptly.

He looked at me sharply, and I thought his face stiffened a little. "Yes, Mr. Sackett, there are. Three or four, I think. All of them big, all of them recently come into the Territory." He paused. "And all of them owned by honorable men."

"That may be, Captain Porter, but one of them saw fit to burn my outfit and try to murder me."

"Perhaps."

"Perhaps? I was there...I lived through it."

"Of course. But what can you prove against anyone? You would have to have proof, Mr. Sackett." He hesitated again. "In a court of law—"

"Captain, I'll find the man. I'll find proof before I act, but when I act I'll be my own law." I stopped him before he could interrupt. "Captain, nobody has more respect for the law than I. We boys were raised up to respect it, but there's no law in the Territory that can reach a big cattleman, and you know it. Not even the Army."

"Mr. Sackett, I must warn you not to take the law into your own hands."

"What would you do, sir?"

He shot me a quick, hard look. "You must do as I say, Mr. Sackett, not as I might if I were in your place." And then he asked, "Why do you suppose they tried to kill you? Why do you suppose your outfit was destroyed?"

"That's what puzzles me, Captain. I just don't know."

He walked to the window and stood there with his hands clasped behind his back. "Was your wife a pretty woman, Mr. Sackett?"

There it was, what had been worrying me all the time, but it was the thing I wouldn't let myself face.

"She was beautiful, Captain, and this isn't just what a man in love would say. She was really, genuinely beautiful. All my brothers would tell you the same. Tyrel, he—"

Porter turned around sharply. "*Tyrel Sackett?*" he was startled. "Tyrel Sackett, the Mora gunfighter, is your *brother?*"

"Yes, sir."

"That would mean that Orrin Sackett is your brother too."

"Yes."

"Orrin Sackett," Captain Porter said, "helped us get a bill introduced in the House. He is a very able man, and a good friend of mine."

"And mighty near as good with a gun as Tyrel, when he wants to be."

He returned to Ange. "Mr. Sackett, I do not wish to offend, but how were things between you and Mrs. Sackett?"

"Couldn't be better, sir. We were very much in love." Right there I told him something of how we met, high in the mountains of Colorado. "If you are suggesting she might have left me, you can think again."

He smiled. "Never, Mr. Sackett. The woman who would leave you would certainly not destroy her wagon or those valuable mules, and you have told me of the money...she would have taken that. No, what I was thinking of was something else.

"Your wife," he went on, "was an attractive woman, and she was alone. This is a country where there are few women, fewer beautiful women."

"Captain, it just doesn't figure. You know how western folks feel about molesting a woman. Nobody'd be fool enough—"

"Suppose he did not stop to think until too late?" Porter walked over to me. "He would have been wild with panic. He would have been desperate to cover up, to remove any possibility of what he had done ever being discovered."

"What about those men hunting me?"

"When you find them I think you will discover they were looking for you for some other reason. I think one man— someone able to command others—is responsible, and only he or they know the real reason you are to be killed."

Of course, it made sense. Also it meant that Ange was dead, and that her death must have been ugly. Suddenly all the fury that was in me came welling up inside until I was almost blind with it. I stood there, my head down, my whole body shaking with it. Inside me there was only one thing left, a terrible will to destroy, to kill.

After a moment I looked up. "Captain, I got to have some rest."

"Al Seiber will take care of you." Porter paused. "Sackett, this conversation is between us. If it is ever mentioned I shall deny that it ever took place. However, in the morning you will have a horse and a mule at your disposal, and I shall speak to Mr. Seiber about the guns."

"I have money. I can buy them."

He nodded. "Of course. But you will want good weapons, and I am afraid what you would find at the sutler's...at the trading post...would not be adequate."

When I stepped outside, he stood in the doorway. It was dark now, and he stood there framed against the light. "Remember, my offer holds. If you want to join up, return here. I am sure I can arrange for your old rank, perhaps for a commission."

After the door closed I stood there a while alone in the darkness. The stars were bright in the desert sky, the night was cold...and Ange, my Ange, was dead.

Suddenly I knew she must be dead, and that all Captain Porter had suggested was true. The chances were her body lay somewhere not far from that wagon.

I was going back to look, to give her a decent burial. And then I was going to hunt a man.

It was a long time before I knew what happened inside that building after I left it...a long, long time.

Captain Porter went to his table and took out a sheet of paper. He put down the place and the date, and then he wrote out a letter and addressed it, a letter that would be in the mail before I ever left the post.

And that letter was to make all the difference to me. Whether it was to be life or death for me was decided by that cavalry captain putting pen to paper in his quiet quarters that night at Camp Verde...but that is another story.

FIVE

One thing I'd learned a long time back. When traveling in enemy country, never return by the same trail you used in going out...they may be laying for you.

Al Seiber told me of an Indian trail that left the Verde at the big bend below Fossil Creek, so I took it and rode across the top of Hardscrabble Mesa and made camp at Oak Spring.

My hands were only partly healed. I could use a rifle well enough, but would hesitate to draw a Colt against anybody. It was two weeks since I'd taken my fall, and I was still in bad shape, but I could wait no longer. Right now I was no more than two miles from Buckhead Mesa and the canyon where the ruins of my wagon lay.

Two to three miles away to the north there was a Mormon settlement—not a town, just a bunch of folks settled in there who had come down from Utah...or so I supposed.

From all I'd heard they were God-fearing folk, and it was there I planned to go when I needed supplies, and it was also where I hoped to get information. For the present what I needed was rest, for I tired easily, and I was still in no condition for what lay ahead.

Oak Spring was a good hide-out. It lay in a canyon, and I'd seen no tracks on the Indian trail leading in here. My good treatment by Victorio, if that was who it was, would mean nothing if I met other Apaches, and the Tontos were some of the worst of the lot.

Over a hatful of fire I made coffee and a good meal, for I had a feeling the meals ahead would be few and far between. At daybreak, back in the saddle, I rode over the mesa, crossed

33

Pine Creek above the canyon and rode back onto Buckhead Mesa.

There were plenty of tracks, most of them at best a week old, all well-shod horses like you'd find on a well-run cow outfit. Nowhere was there the slightest sign there had ever been a wagon on this mesa.

When I reached the site of the burned wagon I got a surprise. Aside from some blackened brush there was no sign there had ever been a wagon here, or a fire. Somebody had done a piece of hard work, doing away with all trace of what had happened. Even the hubs were gone, dragged off somewhere and buried, I figured.

After scouting around and finding nothing, I rode back to where the wagon had been. All the time I was riding with the rifle across my saddle-bows, and keeping a wary eye for riders. I was alone, and how many enemies I had against me I didn't know, but my life wasn't worth a plugged two-bit piece if they found me.

Sitting there by that fire, I was a mighty lonesome man, my heart a-hurting something awful for thoughts of Ange. I'd long been a lonely man before I saw her, and nobody ever had a truer, finer wife.

Being the oldest of the Sacketts, I was first out of the nest when trouble came, and off I'd gone to the war. We were Tennessee folk from the high-up hills, but we had no truck with slavery or looking down the nose at any man. Many a man in my part of the country fought for the South, but while my heart was with her, my head was not, and I rode north to join the Union.

Leaving slavery aside, it was that I was fighting for—the Union. This was my country, and like Sacketts and their kinfolk for many a year, I was ready to take up my rifle and trail it off to the fightin'. Besides, none of us Sacketts were ever much on missing out on a fight. It was just in us to step in and let fly.

So I joined the Sixth Cavalry in Ohio and rode through

the war with them, and then when it was over I started west to seek out my fortune, wherever it should take me.

Tyrel and Orrin had already gone, leaving about the time of the war's end, or just after. They'd gone west seeking a home for Ma, and they found it, and meanwhile Tyrel had won him a name with his shooting and had become a lawman. Orrin, he studied law and had been elected to office.

Here I was with nothing. Ange and me, we had us a gold mine in the high-up Colorado mountains, but getting the gold out was not easy, and we'd have only a couple of months each year in which to work. I'd brought some out, but what I really wanted was a ranch of my own. With what gold I had, I bought some stock and my outfit and we headed west for the Tonto Basin. Now Ange was gone, and my outfit was wiped out, and me...I was a hunted man, sought after by Lord only knew how many. And not a friend to side me but my Colt and Winchester.

Not that there weren't plenty of Sacketts around the country, and we were a feudin' and a fightin' family, but they were scattered wide and far, and no chance for any help to me. There was Lando, Falcon, Tyrel, Orrin, and many another of our name, and all good men.

After I'd put out my fire, I crawled into the place under the trees close to my horse, and there I stretched out my tired body and closed my eyes in sleep.

The sun was high when I rolled out and led the horse to water. Then I left him on a small patch of grass whilst I made coffee and chewed on some jerky. I had a restless, irritable feeling, and I knew what it was. Being a man slow to anger, and one who can fight his anger back for a while, I knew it was working up to a point where all hell would tear loose...and that's no good.

That was the morning I found Ange.

It was only a few rods from where the wagon had been left, and I was scouting around when I saw that crack in the rock. For a moment I stood there, fear climbing up inside me, for all the while my feelings had been fighting against reason, telling me that Ange was still alive, that Ange had somehow gotten away, and that I'd find her.

That crack was no different from others. It was a place where the rocky edge of the mesa had started to break off, and this crack had broken far back into the table rock of the mesa. After a minute I walked over there. Somebody had scooped dirt in there and heaped rock and brush around it. The job had been done in a tearing hurry. Under the brush and the debris, I found Ange.

She had been strangled, but not before she had put up a terrific fight. Her fingernails were stained dark with blood, and there was flesh under them. She had fought, and she had gouged deep.

The bitter cold had left her just as she had been, but I could not bear to look at her face. After what seemed a long time, I got my blanket and wrapped her in it. Then I rode down to where the fire had been; for one thing I'd seen left behind was my shovel. The killer had used it in controlling the fire, and thrown it aside and forgotten it.

Up on the mesa I found a place where the earth was deep and I dug a grave for her, and I buried her there. When it was over I covered the grave with rocks, and then went to work with my new bowie knife and cut a cross for her. Using the heated edge of the shovel, I burned words into this crude cross.

HERE LIES
ANGE SACKETT
MURDERED NEAR THIS SPOT
APRIL 25, 1877

Now whoever had done this would have no doubts. They would know I was alive. But those others, the ones who were hunting me who might not know the truth, they would know it now.

Then I checked my guns again, and mounting up, I rode down off the mesa.

Now the chips were down. They would be hunting me, but I would be hunting them too, and there was no mercy in me. There was only the desire to hunt them down on their bloody trail, and give them a chance to try killing somebody who was not a woman alone.

There wasn't much to Globe in those days, just a few shacks, cabins, and tents scattered along the bank of Pinal Creek. And there were three saloons. I rode up to the first one and swung down, and I saw folks a-looking at me.

Being taller than most, standing six foot three in my socks and somewhat more in boots, I'm accustomed to folks looking at me. But maybe this time there was something else.

In the saloon there were maybe seven or eight men, and I looked around at them. "I'll buy a drink," I said. "I'll buy a drink for the house."

Some of them hesitated, but not for long. A square-jawed man studied me a moment, took up his glass, and looked across it at me. "You aren't celebrating, friend."

"I'm hunting information. I'm looking for a cow outfit that had some hands working the Mogollon country a couple of weeks ago."

Nobody said anything, and finally the man next to me said, "What's the trouble, mister?"

"It's an outfit that has a couple of hands workin' for them named Macon and Dancer."

"You take my advice"—it was a stocky, swarthy-looking man who spoke—"you'll fork that horse of yours and ride out of here."

"I wasn't asking for advice."

The swarthy man grinned at me, but it wasn't friendly. "Why, you damned fool! Macon is the saltiest man with a gun in this country."

"You called me a damned fool."

He put down his glass. "So?"

He was expecting me to reach for my gun, but I couldn't trust my grip, not yet, anyway. So I hit him.

He was almost as tall as me and somewhat heavier—by twenty pounds, maybe. But that first punch counts for a lot, and I meant it to. My left fist smashed him in the teeth, and my right came around and clobbered him on the ear. That ear split and blood started to flow, and he was clawing for a gun, so I reached in and grabbed his belt, jerked him toward me, and then threw him back. He hit the wall with a thud, and when he started to come at me again I gave him a taste of my knuckles in the mouth again, and then both fists in the stomach. He folded up and went down, and I kicked his gun away.

"You talk to me again," I said, "you call me mister."

Then I walked back to the bar and took up my drink.

"That cow outfit," the square-jawed man said, "why are you hunting them?"

The man I'd clobbered was slowly getting off the floor, so I shucked my gun. I couldn't trust myself to draw fast, although I could do all right once it was out. So I just taken it out and held the gun on him and I said, "If you're a friend of Macon's, tell him he didn't kill me the first time. And tell him the next time I'll be looking right at him."

The square-jawed man looked at me from cold, steady eyes. "Are you implying that Sonora Macon shot you in the back?"

With my left hand I removed my hat. They could all see the livid bullet scar, still fresh, with the hair shaved back by the Army surgeon. "I wouldn't know him if I saw him, but he knew my back. He shot me off a cliff up on Buckhead Mesa."

"That's hard to believe."

"You can believe it." I tossed off the rest of my drink and stepped back from the bar. "You can tell them, any of them you see, that I'm hunting them.

"They ran me ragged when I was hurt and unarmed, they

ran me all over that country. But now I'll be running them. You tell any man of that outfit they can fight or hunt a hole, but I'm coming for them."

"You talk large, stranger."

"Anyone that doubts me," I said, "can come asking."

"That outfit has forty men, forty very tough men. Forty good men."

"Good men? Mister, one or more of those men murdered my wife, killed my mules, burned my wagon."

"Killed your *wife?*"

Now there was quiet in the room. Men looked at me, glasses in their hands, all movement stilled by what I had said.

"I left my wife at my wagon and went scouting a way down off Buckhead. Somebody shot at me an hour or so later, then they hunted for my body. I heard them. I heard the names of Macon and Dancer.

"My wife was a good girl. She was strangled, mister, and whoever did it wears her marks on his face. There was blood and torn flesh under her fingernails.

"Then he killed my mules, burned my wagon and the mules, and tried to wipe out all trace of what he had done. He murdered my wife on the twenty-fifth of last month. Mister, there weren't too many men in that part of the country at that time. So I'll find them."

There was a mutter of anger from the men in the room. The square-jawed man's face was white and stiff, but he did not speak. He turned back to the bar. "I'll have another drink," he said thickly.

The bartender rested his hands on the bar. "Anybody who would murder a woman is a no-good skunk. I'll lend a hand with the rope, mister."

One of the men spoke up. "Who might you be, mister? We don't know you."

"I am Tell Sackett," I said, "William Tell Sackett, of Tennessee, Colorado, and a lot of other places."

"You related to the Mora gunfighter?"

"Brother. I taught him to shoot. Although," I added, "he done all right when he taken it up."

The man beside me finished his drink, turned away from the bar, and went outside.

"Who might he be?" somebody asked.

"Cattleman, I guess," another answered. "He's a stranger to me."

Nobody said anything more for a while. Presently the bartender said, "You eaten tonight, mister? You set down over at the table, and I'll fix you up."

Suddenly I was awful tired. My strength was coming back, but that short fight had been too much, too soon. So I leathered my gun and walked over to the table and dropped into a chair.

The bartender brought me food and a pot of coffee, and I thanked him. I ate and drank, but all the while I was thinking of Ange, and away down inside me something burned like a cold fire.

It gnawed away at my insides until there was nothing else in me, nothing to think of, nothing to dream of...only the man I wanted to find, the man I wanted to kill.

Man...or men...There might have been more than one.

SIX

When I'd eaten my fill and drunk my coffee I went outside and stood where the wind came down the draw. It was a wild night, with clouds racing down the long black sky, lighted weirdly by a hiding moon. I stood there alone on what passed for a street, and felt the loneliness and the pain tearing at me.

Ange!...Ange had died horribly and alone, attacked while waiting for me, and never a chance at life, for she had spent her years so much alone before I found her high in those Colorado mountains.

Ange, who was beautiful and tender and thoughtful, who could not bear to see nothing suffer, and who was always thinking of what she could do for me to make my life a happier thing. And little enough of happiness had come my way until Ange came.

Now she was gone, and the thought of it was almost too much for me.

Deep down within me an awful rage was burning. I banked the fires of it and waited, knowing my time would come. My horse turned his head and looked at me in a woebegone manner, for the wind was cold and the night was late, so I went over to him and, taking my Winchester from the scabbard, I stepped into the saddle and walked him down the empty street where dry leaves blew, and the dust.

There was no livery stable in town, only a corral with a few horses standing, tails to the wind. Some boulders and the wall of the mountain made a partial break. So I stripped the leather from him and put it under a little shelter built for the purpose, and then I rubbed him all over with handfuls of grass and turned him into the corral, first standing by while he ate a bit of corn from the sack I carried. It was a small sack, but there was enough to give him the extra something he might need for a long stretch of hard going.

Turning away from the corral, I looked toward the lighted windows. It was late, and this was an early rising town, so it was early to bed. Only a few lights remained, the lights of folks I did not know.

How many such towns had I been in? A lone-riding man is a stranger wherever he goes, and so it had been for me until I met Ange, and so it was again.

There was a bit of a gully where run-off water had cut into the ground, and three times I'd taken care to step over it; but now, so filled I was by my own sorrow, I forgot it. Starting back toward the town I stepped off quickly, put a foot into that ditch, and fell flat on my face...and it saved my life.

When I hit the ground there was the roar of a shot in my ears, and then silence. Me, I just never moved. I lay there quiet, waiting and listening. Whoever had shot at me must have figured I was a dead duck, because he just let me lay. After several minutes had passed and I heard no further sound, I eased myself past the corner of the corral and crouched there, waiting. If anybody was going to risk a first move, it was not going to be me.

After some more time I began to feel sure that my unseen attacker had slipped away quietly and was no longer around. But that was a risk I was not prepared to chance. I backed up and got into some brush at the edge of town and circled wide around until I got back to the saloon. No other place in town had a light.

I pushed open the door and stepped in. There were three men inside.

The bartender looked up at me, and then his eyes sort of slipped over to the man at the end of the bar. Not that I mean that bartender was telling me anything, just that he naturally looked toward that man—probably because that man had come in last.

He was a tall man, but on the slender side, with a narrow, tough face.

Walking up to the bar, I held my Winchester in my right hand, and put my left on the bar. "I'll have rye," I said, and then under cover of the bar, I tilted my rifle muzzle past the corner of the bar and within inches of the tall man's heart. And I held it there.

Nobody could see what my gun hand was doing, but when I took up my drink I looked over at this gent and said, "Somebody took a shot at me out by the corral."

Now, I didn't make a thing of it, I just said it mildly, looking at him. But there was another thing I'd noticed. That man had mud on his boot heels, and the only mud I knew of was alongside the corral where the water trough stood.

He looked right at me. "Wasn't me," he said, "or I'd have killed you."

"I think it was you," I said. "You've got mud on your heels."

His fingers had been resting on the edge of the bar and when his hand dropped for his gun, I squeezed the trigger on my rifle.

That .44 slug knocked him back and turned him half around. I jacked another shell into the chamber and stepped around after him.

He was still standing, but he sort of backed up, going to the wall, and I cat-footed it after him. "Were you one of them that killed my wife?"

He stared at me, looking genuinely puzzled. "Wife? Hell, no. I...I...you tried to kill the boss. Back in the...Mogollons." His words came slowly, and his eyes were glazing.

"He lied to you. You're dying for nothing. Who is your boss?"

He just looked at me, but he never answered, nor tried to answer.

When I faced around to the others, the bartender had both hands resting on the bar in plain sight, and the others the same.

"You took advantage," one of them said.

"Mister," I replied, "my wife was murdered. She was strangled trying to defend herself. My wagon was burned, my mules killed, and forty men spent a week or more combing the mountains to kill me. One of them shot me in the back of the head. I'll play this the way they started it. Wherever they are, whoever they are, they got to kill me, light out of the country, or they'll die—wherever and whenever I find them."

The man gave me a cynical look. "I've heard talkers before."

"Mister, the last feud my family taken part in lasted seventy years. The last Higgins died with his gun in his hand, but he died."

Nobody said anything, so I asked, "Who did he work for?"

They just looked at me. My troubles were my own, and they wanted no part of them, nor could I lay blame to them for it. They were family men and townies, and I had come in out of wild country, and was a stranger to them.

"You might take a look at his horse," the bartender said. "There's likely to be only two at the hitch rail, yours and his."

There had been another horse at the rail when I tied mine, so I turned to the door and started through. A rifle bullet smashed splinters from the door jamb within inches of my face, and I threw myself out and down, rolling swiftly into the shadows with a second bullet furrowing the board-walk right at my side.

In the darkness I rolled back and up to one knee, and I settled myself for a good shot. But nothing happened, nor was there any movement out in the darkness. Two frame buildings and a tent with a floor were just across the street from me; there was also a lot of brush close by, and another corral. I stayed still for several minutes, and then I suddenly thought of that other horse. I went to look, but he was gone.

The horse had been taken away before I came out to the street, but after I had killed the rider in the saloon. And then somebody had waited for me, shooting from the darkness across the street.

Back inside the saloon, the two townsmen were gone...through the back door, no doubt. The bartender was wiping off the bar, taking a lot of time at it.

A pot of coffee stood on the stove and a rack of cups was behind the bar. I picked up a cup, and filled it from the pot on the stove. The place I selected to stand was out of line of any doors and windows.

"I got to do some contemplating about you," I said to the bartender.

He straightened up and gave me a slow, careful look. "About me?"

"You mentioned that horse in the corral. When I stepped to the door I nearly got myself killed."

"If you think I'd set you up—" he began.

"I do think you might if you had reason enough. Now I got to decide what stake you have in this."

He came across to me. "Mister, my name is Bob O'Leary, and I've tended bar from Dodge to Deadwood, from Tombstone to San Antone. You ask anybody, and they'll tell you I'm a man of my word. I've done a few things here and there, and I ain't sayin' what they might be, but I never murdered no woman, nor had anything to do with those that would. Like I told you, you find your man, or men, and I'll lend a hand with the rope...no matter who they be."

"All right, Mr. Bob O'Leary, for the time being I'll take your word for it. All I'll say is your timing was right."

"Nobody needs timing for you, Sackett. You give it some thought, and you'll see your number is up. You stand to be somebody's favorite target.

"Put yourself in his place. Suppose somebody who can

command a lot of men did murder your wife. What's he doin' now? I'll tell you. He's scared...he's scared to death. He's not only scared of you, he's scared of what his own men will believe.

"He's told them a story. He's told them, judging by what that puncher said this evening, that you tried to kill him. They accepted that story. They are all trying to kill you, and you'll have to admit it's more exciting than punching cows.

"Only now you're talking. You're telling a different story, and he's got to shut you up fast.

"Look at it this way," he went on. "That man is riding through the rough country alone. He sees your wife waiting in that wagon. She's a young, pretty woman. Maybe he hasn't seen any kind of a woman in weeks...maybe months. He talks to her, he makes advances and she turns him down. He gets too brassy about it and they start to fight. Upshot is, he kills her. Chances are he had no mind to do such a thing when it all started, but now where is he?

"Mr. Sackett, you got you a scared man. He knows how western folks feel about women. He knows some of his own men would pull on the rope if they knew what he had done. He's sweating with being scared, so he dumps your wagon off a cliff into a place where he doesn't think it will ever be found.

"He's all scratched up, so he calls in some of his hands and tells them you tried to kill him, and he wants you dead. He probably offers a good price, but he wouldn't need to, for riders are loyal—they ride for the brand."

Well, I was listening to all he said. This O'Leary seemed to have it pegged right.

Now he was saying, "He hurries back, he wipes out all the tracks, he goes down and sets fire to your outfit, making sure the wind will take the smoke away from the hunting party. He not only has to wipe out any trace of your outfit, he has to be able to convince anybody that you were just a drifter."

He refilled my cup. "Sackett, let me tell you something.

I don't know who he rides for, but I know this Dancer. He used to come up the trail to Dodge, and he's square. He's a tough man, but he's one to ride the river with."

O'Leary stood there, holding the coffeepot. All the lights in the room were out but one. There was a lamp burning with a reflector behind it, just back of the bar. The light threw dark shadows into the hollows of O'Leary's cheeks.

"I'll tell you something else. He's got Sonora Macon, who is as fast with a gun as any of them, and he's got Al Zabrisky and Rafe Romero...and any one of them would just as soon kill you as not, no matter who you are or what you've done or not done."

I got up and taken my rifle from the table beside me. O'Leary, he went over to the light, cupped one hand at the top of the globe, and then blew into it. The light went out, and the room was in darkness.

"All right, Sackett," he said, "you can go when you are ready."

At the door I stopped. "Thanks," I said, and then I asked, "You don't think I've got a chance, do you?"

"I was always a sucker for lost causes," O'Leary said. "But no—to be honest, I don't think you've got a Chinaman's chance...not with all that outfit against you."

The wind was making up, and dust skittered down the street. It was long past midnight, and the town was dark and silent. When I stepped to the saddle, my horse turned willingly away.

There was no sound but the clop-clop of my horse's hoofs as I rode past the last building and away from town toward the mountains. Avoiding the trails, I took to the mountain slopes and rode away up under the trees. When I was a few miles out, I unsaddled, picketed my horse, and pulled off my boots. Sitting there on my blanket, I rubbed my tired feet and wondered how a man's life could get him into such a spot.

Three weeks back I had me a lovely wife, a brand-new outfit, and I was driving west to settle. Now I had nothing, and was a hunted man.

With my head against my saddle, I leaned back and looked up at the stars I could make out through the pine tops. Right then I found myself wishing I wasn't alone. I kept thinking back to Tyrel and Orrin, wishing for them to be here with me. With those two brothers to side me, I'd tackle hell with a bucket of water.

Sometime about there I dozed off, and in my dreams I was wandering the Tennessee hills again, just as when a boy I had gone picking pods from the honey-locust trees for the making of metheglin, or hunting the wild hogs that ran free along the ridges. In my dreams, there was Ma in her old rocker, a-watching us boys as we worked in the fields, thinking of Pa, she probably was, who had gone off to the westward many a year before. Gone with the mountain men, with Carson, Bridger, Joe Meek, Isaac Rose, and John Coulter.

The long riding had taken it out of me and left my bones with an ache and my muscles sagging with weariness. I was so tired that I slept sound...and then a boot toe took me in the ribs and I was awake, and knew I had awakened too late.

When I looked up, I looked into the blackness of three rifle muzzles, aimed at my head. Three hard men stood over me, no mercy in their eyes.

SEVEN

Oh, they had me all right! Dead to rights, and not a chance to fight back, for even if I could knock one rifle aside, the others would kill me for sure. Yet there was no give in me, for I'd nothing left to lose.

So I lay there without moving or giving them excuse to shoot, and then when I did move it was to lift my hands slowly and clasp them behind my head.

"Cigar in my vest pocket. I'd like to light it," I said.

"Have at it." The speaker was a square-shouldered, well-set-up man of twenty-four or -five. "I'd give any dog a chance for a last smoke."

"If you didn't have that gun on me you'd not call me that. Courage comes cheap when you've got a man hog-tied."

He started to reply, then shut up, but he was mad, I could see that. So I taken my time with the cigar, thinking hard all the while. They looked to be good, solid men.

"You don't look like men who'd murder a woman," I said.

You would have thought I'd laid across them with a whip. "What's that? What d'you mean...who murdered a woman?"

"Your outfit," I said, "maybe some of you. You murdered my wife, and burned everything I had. Now you want to kill me so there won't be anybody to ask questions. That wraps it up, all nice and pretty." I looked up at them. "Except you yellow-bellies will have to live with it the rest of your days."

One of them jerked his rifle up to smash the butt into my face, and if he tried that they were going to have to kill me quick. One of the others held up a hand to stop him...and me, for he saw what was coming.

49

From the way the others reacted I knew I'd hit a nerve, and I waited.

"What's all this about a murdered woman?"

"Who you tryin' to buffalo?" I put all the contempt I had into it. "You know damn' well there ain't five men within a hundred miles, leaving your outfit out of it, who wouldn't pull the rope on a woman-killer. And this was my wife, one of the prettiest, finest women alive."

Well, sir, they just looked at me, but I had them. They were learning something they hadn't known, but maybe what I was saying was answering questions they had been asking themselves.

"I'm Tell Sackett," I said, "and there's places where the name carries weight. I drove in here with a wagon and some fine mules. I drove in with a few head of cattle and a herd following after, and I drove with my wife beside me.

"We hadn't been married but a few months. Sort of a honeymoon, it was. I left her a-setting in our wagon atop Buckhead Mesa and rode off to find a way into Tonto Basin.

"When I was standing on the rim of the mesa above the river, somebody shot me off that mesa and I bounced off rocks and brush all the way down.

"You can see where the bullet struck." I touched the scar on my skull. "I was some stove up, and when I finally got back to where I'd left my outfit it was gone...and so were all the tracks."

Lying there smoking, I talked as I never talked before. I told them of finding my wagon, finding the mules, and afterwards finding Ange. Of the burning, too, and how when I came back again there had been more burning, and even most of the ashes gone. It hurt, talking of Ange, but I kept on.

"Somebody, the man who started you boys on the hunt for me, he killed my wife. And he carries her marks on him....I saw the blood and flesh under her nails. That some-body is purely scared right now. He's got to have me dead, or folks will find out what happened.

"I don't figure," I added, "that he ever expected you to talk to me. I'm laying five to one you were told to shoot me on sight."

Right then I pushed my luck. I knew I had them off balance and trying to figure it out, so I just naturally got up, put on my hat, and then reached for my gun belt.

"Lay off that!" It was that blocky-built puncher again, but I just paid him no mind.

"Go ahead," I said. "A shot at an unarmed man is just what I'd expect of a woman-killer's outfit."

He was white-mad, but like I figured, these men were decent enough. I'd punched cows with a lot like them—good, hard-working men ready for a wild time in town or a shooting fight, but decent men. He didn't shoot, and I slung that belt around me and stood there an armed man, prepared to take my chances with whatever happened.

I'd pushed my luck right out of a corner and into a place where I had a break, anyway. But I wasn't about to stand back and wait.

"You boys were set on me, and you been hunting me high and low. Up to now I don't hold it against you, because you were told some tale to start you. Now you know the truth, and if you keep on a-chasing me, I'm going to start chasing back."

They weren't even listening to what I was saying. One of them turned right around on me. "Was what you said about your wife true?"

"I raised a marker over her grave, and if we were to hunt long enough we could find pieces of that wagon. And I can take you to folks in Globe and away east who knew us and saw us headed west."

"You were in Globe?"

"My wife and me, we spent two days and nights in that town just three weeks ago come Sunday."

They swapped looks, and I could see that meant something to them, but I wasn't sure what. That tough young puncher, he all of a sudden stood his rifle down and dug into his shirt pocket for the makings. "I don't know about you fellers," he said, "but I've got a feelin' I'd be better off in Texas."

A thought came to me. "About Globe, now. Were you boys in that town three weeks ago?"

"Yeah…the whole shootin' outfit. We spent several days there. Fact is, we were supposed to stay longer, but then we got orders to move out, sudden-like, on Monday morning."

That had been the morning we left.…Suddenly I was remembering three men who had ridden past our wagon, and one of them had turned to look back at Ange.

The same man had been buying supplies at the same time we were. I tried to place him, but all I could remember was that he was a big man.

Well, I was hungry, and a man isn't going to go far on an empty stomach. Not that I hadn't put miles behind me without food, but right now I had it with me to cook, and I was hungry as a Panhandle coyote. So I put coffee water on the fire and said, "You boys might as well set up. You got something to think about, and this here's as good a place as any."

They moved up to the fire, and I went rousting through my duffle, getting out the bacon and the rest. Then I looked around at them and asked, innocent-like, "Who d' you boys ride for?"

They just looked at me. They might not like what I'd told them, but they weren't going to sell out their boss. They were good men. Only they didn't need to tell me, and maybe they thought of that, too. All I had to do was look past them at the brands on their horses—a capital A lying on its side…*Lazy A.*

There had been cattle with that brand in some of the country I'd ridden through, and there had been a horse of that brand at the hitch rail of the saloon when I first rode up to Globe after leaving Camp Verde.

A cattleman or any rider in range country just naturally notices any brand he sees on the stock along the way. He has cattle on his mind, and brands are one of the biggest parts of his job.

Over coffee one of these gents suddenly said, "We got no call to believe what you said, only something about this here has a smell we don't like. You don't size up like any dry-gulching killer. I got a feelin' you been talking truth."

"All I ask," I said, "is not to stand in my way."

"There's some that will."

Evidently they had no news from Globe, so I decided to let them have it, and now. "One tried," I said, "last night down to Globe."

I told them about it, and when I finished they sat still for a moment or two, and then one of them said, "I mind that gully."

"Andersen," another said, "Curly Andersen."

"He was close on to bald."

"I know. That's why we called him Curly. Well, maybe he would try it that way. You beat him to the draw?"

"Mister," I said, "when it comes to fighting, a body makes up his own rules with me. I'll fight him fair as long as he shows himself of a like mind. This Curly Andersen tried to ambush me, so he laid out the rules and I played according."

Reaching for the pot, I filled my cup, then the cups of the others.

"Only maybe he figured *I'd* made the rules. He said I'd tried to ambush his boss back in the Mogollons. Anyway, he drew cards in a tough game."

When they had gone, I saddled up and rode out of there, making it a policy never to stay too long in one place when I knew I had enemies, and especially when they had me located.

All the time I was keeping my thoughts away from Ange. Whenever she came to mind I felt a vast, aching emptiness inside me, and a loneliness such as not even I had ever known.

Three days passed, three days of riding and resting, three days of prowling like a lonely wolf, pushing my horse down old trails and finding new ones through rock and brush and butte. And all the while I was working out the trails of those who hunted me, and of the Lazy A cattle, slowly tracing out the maze they made to find my way to their headquarters.

It was a high and lovely country. I rode through broken land crested and ridged with pines, with beautiful meadows and streams that rushed along over stones with a happy chuckling sound. Cold water it was, from fresh-melted snow.

My strength was building back, and I took good care to give my horses rest and to stake them each night on good grass. Each time I made myself a fire I ate at that spot, and then moved on for a mile or two, camping in some unlikely place, and wiping away all traces of my camp when I left. And every day I varied my way of going, wanting to weave no pattern they could read.

More and more I was finding horse tracks, and I knew I was getting closer. My enemy had men beside him, and I rode alone. My enemy had spare horses, and many eyes with which to seek me out, and I had only two. But there was Indian in my nature if not in my blood, and I hunted my way across country like a ghost, only the butt of that Colt was near my hand, and my rifle ready for use. Sometimes I made dry camp, chewing on jerky or a crust of bread, and always I avoided human beings.

It was a month to the day of the time Ange had been killed when I saw the strange rider.

The weather had turned bad, and I had found a deep hollow under an overhang near the top of the ridge that divided Cibecue Creek from Carrizo Creek. It was wild and lonely here, with only the ghost of an old trail along the ridge that showed no signs of travel, none at all. The trail might have been made a hundred years ago, judging by its vagueness. But in arid country, or even on the lonely ridges in forested country, such trails, used long ago by Indians, seem to last forever.

Thunder rumbled above the rim, dark now with forest and with the impending storm, and a few scattering drops of cold rain fell. The shelter I had was good, although higher on the ridge than I liked, even though the rim towered almost a thousand feet higher three or four miles to the north.

A man riding wild country never stops looking for camping spots. If he doesn't use them at the time, he may next week or next year, or five years later. It is one of those unconscious things a body takes to when riding free of towns and ranches.

The place I'd found was deep under the overhang, masked by some brush, and I'd heaved a couple of rock slabs up to make added shelter. My horse couldn't get into it, but I found him a place under the trees where intersecting branches made cover of a kind.

Before me the ground broke away into the canyon of the Carrizo, and as I looked down the canyon I saw the rider, who drew rein, turned in the saddle, and looked carefully around, like a man who is lost.

I could guess what happened, and it didn't take a lot of figuring. That rider had mistaken the Carrizo for the Cibecue, for back up where the two canyons headed up they weren't more than a couple of miles apart, maybe even less. And there was one branch of the Cibecue that began only a couple of hundred yards from the Carrizo. Somebody not used to the country might easily mistake the one for the other.

That rider was in trouble, for the two canyons ran parallel to each other for only a few miles, and the further down the canyon he rode...no, *she* rode, for by that time I was positive the rider was a woman...the further down the canyon she rode, the further she would get from where she was going.

Suddenly lightning flashed and thunder crashed, and the rider's horse reared up and bolted. And then the rain came...it came hard, and in a real old back-country gully-washer. The rider disappeared below the walls and out of my sight, her horse running wild and crazy in the kind of country where a horse would do well to walk.

The rain drew a gray veil across the landscape, a veil like shimmering steel, that shut out the crags, shut out the darkness of the pines, and started big drops falling over the edge of my overhang.

Here I was snug and dry, but I was unquiet in my mind, for I was thinking of that woman, her horse running away over wet rocks in a wild canyon. If she could stay with the horse and he didn't break his fool leg or her neck, they would be all right. Only I didn't think for a minute she would get through.

I sat there maybe ten minutes, secure in my hideaway, with the rain falling outside. The canyon, I knew, was going to be running belly-deep for a tall horse within the next couple of hours...maybe sooner. If anybody was down, but conscious, they might have a chance; unconscious, anybody down there on the ground would be dead.

Finally I got up, cussing myself for being a damned fool to go off a-helping somebody in a country full of enemies.

When I slung a saddle on my horse he gave me a hurt look. He was as tired of it all as I was, and I hadn't my strength back. I had figured to sit right where I was and rest up a couple of days while my enemies worried about where I was.

I found her, and sure enough, she had fallen or been thrown from the saddle. She was lying among the rocks, her face white as all get-out, her black hair spilled around her on the wet sand.

Her horse was fifty yards off, standing three-legged with the saddle under his belly. When I walked over to get the horse and fix the rig up, I saw that he'd gone lame. The leg wasn't broken, but it was hurt, and that horse wasn't going to carry anybody very far, not for a while.

So I led him back to where the lady lay, and I picked her up and slung her over my shoulder and heaved her aboard my own horse. Holding her on the saddle in front of me, I returned to the overhang and my fire.

When I put her down beside the fire she opened a pair of the deepest, blackest eyes I had ever seen, and she said, "Thank you, Mr. Sackett. I was afraid I would never find you."

EIGHT

Now I was never no hand with womenfolks. Mostly when
I went to dances back in the Tennessee hills I went for
the fighting that went on between times or after. Orrin, that
brother of mine who was a hand to sing and play the fiddle,
he could talk to women. Those Trelawney gals back there
were always a-taking after him, but he had a way that could
charm the prissiest ones into walking out with him. Seemed
like he knew every pretty girl from Cumberland Gap to the
Highland Rim.

Here was I, a long homely man and no hand to talk,
rained into an overhang cave on a Tonto ridge with one of
the prettiest little girls you ever did see, and the trails buried
stirrup-deep under rushing water. The way she looked up at
me, I was almighty sure she was less put out than me.

"What do you mean, ma'am? And how did you know
me?"

She was lying there beside the fire, looking as cute as
a cub 'coon in a hollow tree, and she seemed in no mind to
sit up, although I was fairly a-sweating, wishing she would.

"There's no man anywhere so tall," she said, "or so
strong. My! You picked me up as if I was a baby!"

Well, she wasn't any baby. She was little, but she was
doing her share where it counted, judging by the way she
shaped out her clothes.

"Now see here. I'm not fixed to take care of any woman.
I'm a foot-loose, long-riding man, and when this storm is over,
you go back to your ma."

"I don't have one."

She gave me a woe-begone look that would have curled

my socks, if I'd owned any. I just shoved my bare feet down into my boots.

"And if you keep on I won't have any father, either," she said.

That set me back. So I made up to work over the fire. Only thing wrong with it, that horse of hers wasn't wearing any Lazy A brand. The horse had followed along, limping up the mountain after us, and he was standing under the trees with my two horses.

"How did you expect to find me?"

She sat up and locked her hands around one knee. "By just riding. Only I got lost, somehow."

That didn't make any impression on me. I went about fixing up a bite of something to eat, knowing nobody would smell smoke in all that rain, and probably nobody would be riding until it was over. Nonetheless, I kept an eye on the country around, not really believing this girl was out alone. But the rain was going to wash out any tracks, and anybody hunting me was going to have to wait until I started moving again, or until this girl told it around that she'd seen me.

All the while I fussed over the fire, I was thinking over the business of this girl showing up. Now, this Mogollon country was *wild*. Over here where I was now, over half the country stood on end, and it was crags and boulders, brush and fallen trees. It was really rough, and no place a body would be likely to find a hot-house flower like this girl. She had soft hands and soft skin, and showed little sign of being out much in wind and sun. She could ride, all right, but she was no cow-country girl. Leastways, she hadn't been for some time. If such a girl was in this country at such a time, she was bait for something. And who was everybody fishing for? Me.

The best thing I could do was get shut of this girl as fast as I could, but I surely couldn't drive her out in the rain. Yet the more I thought of it, the uneasier I became. From time to time I sneaked a look at her. She was in no way upset by being caught with a strange man in wild country. She was young, all right, maybe not more than seventeen or eighteen, but there was a kind of wise look about her eyes that made me think that, girl-wise, she'd been up the creek and over the mountain. I began to think that killing me wasn't enough. Now they were fixing to get me hanged.

Making coffee and broiling a couple of venison steaks took little time. Whilst we ate that, and the last of my bread, I figured out what I was a-going to do.

By the time we'd finished eating, the last of the light was going. Maybe I was wrong, but I wasn't going to chance it. I stowed away my eating gear and taken up my saddle. She sat up straight then and looked at me.

"What are you going to do with that?" she asked.

"Put it near my horse," I said, "case I have to light out fast before morning. I always stow my gear where I can lay hand to it."

She couldn't see what I was doing back under the trees, and when I was saddled and packed, I walked back to the overhang. "Ma'am," I said, "you—"

"My name is Lorna," she interrupted.

"All right, ma'am." I stood a good country distance off from her. "I got to look off down the valley. If anything happens I don't get back, you just follow that creek." I indicated the Cibecue. "It will take you down to the flat land."

"Mr. Sackett"—she looked so almighty lonesomelike I almost changed my mind...almost—"Mr. Sackett, I am most afraid. Won't you stay with me?"

Well, I swung a leg over my saddle. "Ma'am," I said, "you get scared, 'long about midnight you let out a scream and you'll have all kinds of company. You'll have those boys you got waiting back up there in the trees...they'll come a-running."

Then I grinned at her. "Miss Lorna, you scream. I'll bet they'll be mighty surprised when they find you alone."

With that I touched a spur to my horse and went off down the trail toward the Cibecue. Then I doubled back and rode into still rougher country.

It was graying toward light on a wet, still morning when

I finally found a place to hole up. It was right under the Tonto Rim, soaring more than a thousand feet above me, near a spring that showed no human, horse, or cow tracks—a sort of natural shelter made by trees falling off the rim and piling up on the rocks. And right there I sat tight for three days.

It was plain enough what they had tried to do. That girl's fall was more than likely the real thing, but the idea was to have her up there with me, and then during the night she would begin to scream and they would come down there and find us together. I'd be hanged right on the spot, and any story I'd told previous would be put down as so many lies. Or they'd claim I got rid of my own wife and tried to lay it to somebody else. I hadn't let her know what I was going to do until I was in the saddle, and if she started screaming then it wasn't going to do much good. I never did hear tell of a man attacking a woman a-horseback.

There was reason to sit still here, for I had some studying to do. It was time to sit and contemplate.

All the while I figured I'd lost them and was riding off scot-free, they had known where I was. They had known right where I stopped and they had that girl ready. For now it wasn't enough just to kill me—they had to scotch that story I'd told of my wife's murder.

But how had they known where I was?

The only way I could figure it, was that they had all the trails watched, and maybe some way of signaling, like the Army heliograph they were using against the Indians. As soon as I'd taken direction, they could begin to concentrate until they had me pegged right to a spot.

And if that was so, they must know where I was now...or just about where. They might be closing in on me, surrounding me even now.

When I got to this point in my figuring, I came up off that ground fast. I taken up my rifle and a bag of extra shells and moved out to get my horses...but the horses were gone!

Slipping back into my shelter, I picked up what coffee and grub I could carry, took my blanket and poncho, made a quick bundle and a back pack, and then eased out into the open.

What were they fixing to do? They had my horses, what were they waiting for? Maybe for the man who wanted me dead. Maybe he wanted to see me die.

Standing close against a tree, I studied the lay of the ground about me. Right back of me a steep, brush-choked canyon led to the top of the rim. All around there were trees and brush, and the woods were silent...too silent for a place where there were squirrels and birds.

Every instinct told me they were out there, that they had me where they wanted me, and this time they did not intend to fail. If I went forward they would be waiting and they would take me, and hang me or shoot me; but what if I moved back, up that brush-filled canyon to the rim?

Then it came to me that that was just what they wanted me to do, that up there, others would be waiting for me.

Cold sweat was on my body, cold fear in my heart. I was downright scared. There was nothing in me that was ready to die...at least, not until I found the man or men who murdered Ange.

But it had to be one of the two. There was no other way. To go down the slope into the trees was surely death; to go up the canyon was maybe death. Me, I chose the maybe. Like a ghost I slipped from tree to tree, working my way back and up. Here they had no lookouts, here they could see no further and no better than me, or maybe even less well, for I was like an Indian in the woods...I'd spent time with them back in Tennessee.

Once I got into the mouth of the canyon it meant climb, for this was a run-off canyon, cut by water falling from the Mogollon Rim. That rim was up, almost two thousand feet in places.

Thick stands of pine grew along both walls, and among them it was a tangle of brush and fallen trees. The going was a nightmare, and sometimes it was easier to crawl. Down below me I heard a long call, as if somebody down there was signaling to someone up above. And after a while I heard a call from the right, but down below.

It came to me that I didn't have to keep going up—I could go along the face of the canyon wall. Mostly it was covered with thick brush and trees, but in places it was bare rock. A wild, rugged place it was, home for rattlers, cougars, bobcats, and eagles, and no place at all for a man.

Suddenly a branch ripped my shirt. I stopped, sweating and listening, but there was no sound. Yet I knew they were there. I changed direction, easing off toward the left.

The mountain fell away below me and loomed up far above. Each step had to be taken with the greatest care, and each one seemed a dreadful hazard. It seemed almost certain that they were going to get me. I might kill one man, I might kill three or four, but there was an almighty slim chance that I could win out in the end.

Once, skirting a huge rock to which I clung with one hand, the ground gave underfoot, and it was only that I grabbed quick and caught hold of a bush that saved me. The bush started to tear free, but I threw myself forward and got a fresh grip on the rock.

I knew that there were places where I could fall five or six hundred feet, and though in other places I might not fall more than ten, almost everywhere there were jagged rocks or broken-off trees that I would fall on.

I kept on, and sometimes I stopped to rest, panting like a winded horse. My shirt was soaked with perspiration. It was coming on to sundown, and I feared the oncoming night. And I was thinking that by now they either guessed that I was going along the wall or they figured I had stopped somewhere in the canyon.

Presently I saw ahead of me a bare stretch, swept clean by a rock slide. It was a ragged, ugly slope where I would have to work my way across, depending on my hands. If I could get across there, I might find a place to sit down or lie down. Only there for a little space I'd be clean in the open.

My Winchester was hanging by a crude sling from my

shoulder, butt up, barrel hanging near my right hand. With infinite care, I put my foot out and down. The rock was solid. It was like crossing a stream on stepping stones, only if these stones gave way, I'd fall a couple of hundred feet.

Me, I was shaking. Twice rocks moved under my feet, and I left them just in time to keep from falling.

Then, when I was almost across, there came the sudden wicked *whap* of a bullet striking near me. Involuntarily I ducked and slipped, catching myself by my hands.

Down there in a clearing, maybe three hundred yards below, I saw the man taking sight on me. He had me dead to rights against that slope, but the light was none too good for him.

One foot braced below me, one knee pressed into a notch of the wall, I grasped my rifle by the barrel and swung it up, my left hand taking the barrel, my right hand going back to the action.

He was standing in the clearing, full in the light. An instant I steadied the rifle, taking up slack on my trigger, and then my rifle jumped in my hands just as he fired. My bullet struck him the instant he shot, because I saw him throw up his rifle, the streak of fire from the muzzle clear in the growing shadows, and then he fell, and the sound of our shots went racketing off against the great crags, and then it was still. The shots had been so close together that they were almost one.

He didn't move. He just lay there, and I held myself still and watched. Score one for me. Now they knew they weren't in this for fun.

When a man takes up guns in fighting, somebody is going to get hurt. Somehow folks mostly think it will be somebody else, but we're all vulnerable, and nobody has a free ride. With guns, you pay to learn, only sometimes you learn too late.

By the time I was on the other side among the trees nobody had come to him, but they would. They would find him there, and they would be able to read the future for some of them.

Just before dark I found a place where deer or other game had walked, a tiny path not over three or four inches wide, hanging above a black gulf. It gave me speed, and I followed it as long as it went straight ahead, but when it turned down slope, I gave it up.

That night I slept behind a log that had fallen along the face of the cliff and lay wedged in the rocks. There was a thin space between the face of the rock and the log, but it wasn't wide enough for a man to fall through. So I just rolled my blanket around me and slept there until daybreak.

When I woke, my first thought was: They had hunted me—now they would see what it meant to be hunted.

NINE

There was a poker game going in Uncle Ben Dowell's saloon in El Paso. The night was quiet and business was slow. The stage had pulled in and gone, and most of the loafers had departed for their beds. From somewhere down the street came the faint sound of a piano.

Nobody in the saloon was a stranger. The drummer who had just walked in and put down his valise could scarcely be called that...he had been in El Paso before.

The dark, powerfully built man with the mustache and three scars on his face was not exactly a stranger, either. He had been in El Paso for three days, and the way people were coming and going in this town that practically made him a resident.

That dark man was no kind of a talker, so nobody knew where he was from or where he was going. He had come into town riding a mule, which was strange enough, and riding beside him was the long-jawed, yellow-eyed man with the gold earrings in his ears who was tinkering now with Uncle Ben's clock.

Nobody said anything until the drummer had a drink. "There's hell to pay in the Mogollons," he said when he had put his glass down. "The Lazy A outfit has forty men hunting a man in the wild country under the rim. They'll get him, too."

"Good outfit," Uncle Ben commented. "I know them."

"You *knew* them," the drummer said. "All the old hands have quit, and they've taken on gunmen and man hunters. Only one man against them, and he's running them ragged."

"What started it?"

"Sackett claims his wife was murdered by someone in the Lazy A outfit, and he's sworn to find the murderer. He's—"

The dark man with the scarred face turned his head. "Did you say *Sackett?*"

The drummer looked at him and nodded. "That's right. They say he's Tell Sackett, brother to that Mora gunfighter."

The dark man pushed his chips to the center of the table. "Buy me out," he said. "I'm leaving."

"Look here," a player protested, "you're winning. You can't leave now."

The man stood up. "I'm leaving. You want a chance for your money, you follow me to Arizona."

The tinkering man took up the clock and carried it to the bar. "There you are, Mr. Dowell. It ain't working, but I'll be back this way and do the job right for you."

There was silence in the room when they left, and then somebody said, "Now what started all that?"

Ben Dowell jerked his head to indicate the drummer. "He mentioned a Sackett in trouble. Well, that was Orlando Sackett and his saddle partner, the Tinker."

"What's that mean?"

"It means the Lazy A better hire more men. Forty's not going to be anywhere near enough."

The lone sheepherder paused on the knoll to let the rest of the flock drift past him. He watched his dogs for a minute or two, then his eyes were drawn to the west. The sun was just below the horizon and the red rock cliffs were weirdly lit. Out of the west a tiny puff of dust lifted, grew, and became a fast-running horse.

The rider pulled up, his horse rearing with the sudden stop. "Howdy, Mex! You got any grub to spare? I'm a right hungry man."

"*Si, Señor.*" He pointed toward his camp. "There are frijoles."

The rider wheeled his horse and walked him toward the camp. As they came near the spring the horse tugged toward it, but his rider held him back. "You take it easy, boy. Cool off a mite."

He dropped the reins and walked toward the fire where the blackened coffeepot stood.

The Mexican looked thoughtfully at the horseman. He was a big man, towering well above the Mexican, and he was strongly made. His nose had been broken in more than one fight, and there was a wild, reckless, uncurried look about him.

His black hair hung around his ears, there was a bullet hole in the crown of his hat. He wore two guns, and wore them tied down for action. His buckskin shirt was dark from dust and sweat. His boots were run down at the heel, but he wore jingling spurs with huge rowels, California spurs.

He glanced toward the sheep pens and the corral beyond where several horses stood. "You own those horses?"

"No, Señor. The *patrón*."

"Who's he?"

"Don Manuel Ochoa. He is in Santa Fe, Señor."

"Tell him Nolan Sackett needed a horse. I'm taking the sorrel."

The sheepherder looked again at the shaggy, unkempt rider and the guns. "*Si, Señor*. I will tell him."

When Nolan Sackett went to catch up the sorrel and switch saddles, the sheepherder looked in the bean pot. It was empty. So was the coffeepot, and the tortillas were gone too.

Nolan Sackett walked the sorrel back to camp to make the change of saddles, and then dug down in his pocket and took out a four-bit piece. He glanced at the half-dollar.

"Mex," he said, "that's all I got, but I owe you for the grub. It was mighty tasty."

"You owe me nothing, Señor. I am honored." The Mexican hesitated, and then said, "You are a brother to *Señor* Tyrel, perhaps?"

"Cousin, you might say." Nolan glanced quizzically at the sheepherder. "You know Tyrel?"

"No, Señor, but it is known that he is a good man, and a friend to Mexicans." The sheepherder paused. "Señor, the half-dollar...it is not much." He hesitated again. "Would the señor...perhaps a loan?" He extended a gold eagle.

Nolan Sackett, whom not many things could astonish, was astonished now—astonished and touched. He looked at the old Mexican. "You don't know me, old man. And I might never come this way again."

The old man shrugged.

"I can't lay claim to goodness, old man. I'm a Clinch Mountain Sackett, and we've the name of being rough folk. I never paid much mind to where money came from as long as I had it to hand, but nobody ever loaned me any, not as I recall. I'm obliged."

He tightened the cinch, then swung to the saddle. "Thanks, old man. And if somebody comes by, you tell them to ride high-tail to Mora and tell Tyrel and them that a Sackett's in trouble in the Mogollons."

The pound of the horse's hoofs became a lessening sound in the still mountain air. The old Mexican looked after the rider, long after he had disappeared from sight, and then he said, "Vaya con Dios!"

In the shadowed coolness of the ranch house on Mora Creek the dining-room table was laid for ten, and as the Mexican girls moved swiftly and silently about, making last-minute preparations for dinner, their skirts rustled with excitement. Orrin Sackett was up from Santa Fe after his return from Washington, D.C.

Tyrel Sackett, wearing a black broadcloth suit, sat in a big hide-covered chair listening to Orrin.

The huge living room was two stories high, and was framed by a balcony on three sides with a beautiful staircase leading to the upper floor. The room itself was sparsely furnished and cool.

"Cap should be here any minute, Orrin. He rode out this morning to check the range on the south."

"How is Cap?"

"You know how he is. He's lived all his life on beef, beans, and gun smoke. If somebody doesn't shoot him, he'll live forever."

"Heard from Tell?"

"Never a word since they left for Arizona. I've held back the herd, waiting. But you know Tell...he was never any hand to write."

"Look, Tye, I can't tell you how important this meeting is. Ollie Shaddock is coming over, and the men with him want me to run for the United States Senate. It's a big step, and I'd like to try."

"What do they want from me?"

"Tye, the Mexican vote can elect me, and you know as well as I do that most of them do not trust Anglos, and they know very little about them. They do know something about me...or you.

"What's important is that they believe in you—they know you, and they like you. What the men back of me want is your assurance that you're supporting me. And they want you to tell some of your Mexican friends."

Tye laughed. "Damn it, Orrin, who else would I support? You're not only my brother, but an honest man. Sure, I'll drop the word, but it isn't necessary. They remember you, and they trust you. Believe me, the only mistake your friends are making is in underrating the political sense of the Mexicans. They aren't easily led, and they certainly aren't easily stampeded."

"I'll need the help, Tye. There's a lot of talk against electing a gunfighter to the Senate—or to any public office."

"You mean they've forgotten about Andy Jackson?" Tyrel said. "Or Thomas Hart Benton? And Cassius Clay, our ambassador to Russia?"

He crossed his legs. "Anyway, Orrin, you weren't the one who got into gunfights. I was the one."

The door opened suddenly, and Drusilla, breathtakingly lovely, stood framed there. "Tye, it's Cap. He's got bad news."

Cap Rountree stepped past her. "Tye, a Mexican boy just rode in. There's word that Tell's in trouble. The whole Lazy A has taken in after him and they've got him cornered back in the breaks under the Mogollon Rim. They're going to hang him, Tye."

Tyrel Sackett knocked the ash from his Spanish cigar and placed it carefully on the ash tray. "Cap, have them saddle a horse for me."

He turned to Orrin. "Sorry. You can tell them for me that I'm with you...all the way...when I get back."

"Dru will have to tell them. I'm going along."

"Tye," Cap interrupted, "this here's worse than you think. Somebody killed Ange, and the whole lot of old hands on the Lazy A up an' quit. What they've got now are a passel of border gunmen."

"There's the three of us," Orrin said to his brother, "you, me, and Tell."

"Four," Cap said. "Since when have I missed a Sackett fight?"

It was past midnight when the stage rolled up to Knight's Ranch, and the few passengers got down stiffly. The tall, elegant man who helped his lovely wife from the coach looked unrumpled, showing no evidence of the long, chilling, and dusty ride. Nor did she.

"Better grab a bite to eat, folks," the driver advised. "Doubt if you'll get anything worth eatin' this side of Globe."

The tall man offered his wife his arm and together they went to the door of the thick-walled adobe ranch house that doubled as a stage station. Inside, it was warm and comfortable. The table was freshly laid, with a white cloth and napkins...unheard of in western stage stations.

As they stepped through the door, he heard a rattle of hoofs on the hard-packed earth, and turned to look back. Something in the appearance of the two riders arrested his attention.

"Gin, you've been asking me what the mountain people back home look like."

She came back to stand beside him, watching the two tall, long-legged men dismount from their cow ponies. Neither was more than twenty years old, and they were built alike, lean and big-boned. Each carried a rifle as if it were part of him, and they dressed in worn homespun. "Right out of the hills, Gin."

"Falcon, look at them. At their faces."

"Yes, I see what you mean. At least, there's a possibility."

As the two men came through the door, dusty and travel-worn, he turned to them. "Gentlemen? If I may suggest a drink."

They paused, studying him with frank curiosity. Then the older one of the two said, "We'd take that kindly, mister, kindly."

Falcon turned to his wife. "If you will excuse us, Gin?"

The three walked to the bar, and Gin Sackett looked after them, amused.

Tall and lean, the three men stood up to the bar. A girl came from the kitchen and placed a bottle and glasses before them.

"Gentlemen," Falcon said when they had poured, "your health!"

When they had placed their empty glasses back on the bar, he commented, "A fine flavor, gentlemen, although it lacks the taste of the metheglin."

The two exchanged a glance. "I knowed it. Sure enough, I said, a man with a face like that would have to be a Sackett from the Tennessee mountains. Where y'all from?"

"It's been a while," Falcon said. "I'm Falcon Sackett. Tennessee, North Carolina, points west and south."

The taller one, who had a scar on his cheekbone, said,

"I'm Flagan Sackett. This here's m'brother, Galloway. We come fresh from the hills, and then last night we heard talk."

"Talk?"

"There's a Sackett ridin' ahead of trouble in the Mogollons. We'uns are Sacketts. So we're ridin' to the Mogollons."

"I hadn't heard."

"Talked about a good bit. Seems he claims some fellers killed his wife when he was off scoutin' trail. He's fetched in after them. Only there's maybe forty of them and one of him, and they've got him treed."

"We'll have to ride hard," Falcon said. "You comin', mister?"

"I'm with you. But we may be too late."

"He couldn't be so ornery. Not even a Sackett could be so down-right ornery. He don't dare let us be late."

"Ornery?"

"He couldn't be so ornery as to kill all forty of 'em before we get there."

Flagan put down his glass, glanced regretfully at the bottle, and moved swiftly from the bar.

TEN

When I opened up my eyes there on the face of that cliff I was a sore and hungry man. There was in me a craving for coffee, and a burning ache to get at those men down below. But first I had to find a way off the cliff where they had me treed.

There was an ugly feeling in me against those men and whoever had killed Ange. It was me or them, with all the advantage on their side. They knew this country better than me, and there was more of them. All the same, I was going to make them pay the price. They'd bought chips in my game, but I was going to spin the wheel.

Slinging my rifle so's my hands would be free, I started along the face of the cliff, and it was getting steeper and steeper. Here and there I hung just by my fingers, and once I had to close my fist and jam it in a crack and hang by it to keep from falling.

And all the while that skittish, scared feeling that they would come upon me while I hung out there against the bare rock. Only they didn't—not right then, at least.

Then, all of a sudden, I saw a ledge about eight feet below me, a ledge not more than a couple of feet wide, and below it the cliff fell sheer away. But it was better than where I was, and I took a chance and let go.

I landed right on the edge on my toes and felt the rock crumble underneath my feet, but I lay hold of a bush and worked myself over to a solid section of the ledge. It was the edge of a strata of sandstone, with limestone over it that had weathered back, and it gave me another chance to make time...up to a point.

Crawling around a slight curve, I suddenly found myself facing a full-grown mountain lion that had been coming my way. We stood there, not over ten feet apart, looking each other right in the eye.

He laid his ears back and snarled, but you don't find any bigger coward anywhere than a mountain lion. All the same, if he gets hurt he goes crazy mad. His brain is just one white-hot drive to kill, so what I had to do was bluff that cat, because if I hurt him that would be the end for me right there.

So we stood there a-staring at each other, hating each other, and trying to outprove each other. My rifle was hung by its sling, and the thong was slipped over my .45, so the best I could get at in a hurry was my bowie knife. That old bowie was honed down to shave with, and I could lop off that cat's head with a swipe of it...if he didn't get me first.

"Beat it, cat," I said. "I want no truck with you."

He snarled at me, turning his head and avoiding my eyes, and I had no choice but to wait him out. He might go back, but there was no going back for me. At last he did back off and turn, but I didn't move after him. I was perfectly willing to let that lion go.

Then I smelled smoke.

Crouching down on the ledge to make myself small, I gave study to the country below me and around. Away up ahead of me, several miles off, was a projecting point, and if my figuring was right, somewhere between that point and me was the Tonto Trail. And down below in the pines was a campfire—a thin trail of smoke came up from the trees down there.

The face of the rim was less steep where I now was. An agile man could work his way up or down, and there was plenty of cover. So I decided to make them trouble.

I unslung my Winchester and studied that smoke. Men would be gathered around it, and it was likely they were the men hunting me. Only I didn't know that for sure, and any man who shoots at a sound or at any target he cannot see clearly is taking a big chance.

As I squatted there on the ledge I realized that what I needed most of all was some grub and a horse, my own horse if I could find him. The grub I had in my pack, and I dug into the grub sack for a chunk of frying-pan bread and some jerked meat. I ate it, longing for a drink of anything to wash it down. The closest place I could think of to get it was right down there where that smoke was. I put the back of my hand across my mouth to get any stray crumbs, and then I went down the cliff through the trees.

By the time I reached the bottom of the cliff, I was only a hundred yards or so away from the camp. It was in the cool of morning. Dew sparkled on the grass, and the leaves of the low brush dripped with it. Birds were singing and fussing around in the brush, and in one place I saw the tracks of a big cougar...maybe the one I'd seen on the trail above. I worked my way along, Injun-like, making a sort of rough half-circle around the camp to see how the land lay.

First off, I located the horses, mine among them. Then I went on, getting closer and closer, and all the while studying how I could get away if the going got rough.

I saw that most of the men were gathered close around the fire. I got within fifty feet of their circle when one of them stood up to fill his cup from the coffeepot and, looking across the circle, saw me. For an instant he just stood there, and then he dropped his cup and grabbed for his gun. I broke his arm with a bullet from my Winchester.

Now, I won't say I was trying for his arm. As a matter of fact, I had that rifle dead-center on his shirt button about two inches above his belt buckle, but his quick move turned him so he wound up with a busted wing, and you never saw such a quiet bunch of men.

"No need for anybody to get theirselves killed," I said conversationally, "although I'm in no way particular."

Nine of them were there, but the man with the broken arm was in no mind to cause further trouble.

"Saw your smoke," I said, "and figured I'd drop in for breakfast. Now just to make sure I'm welcome, you boys sort of unbuckle. I'm not going to give any warnings. If any of you feel like taking a chance, you'll never find a better time to die. It's a right pretty morning."

You never saw so many delicate fingers. Those boys unbuckled so carefully you'd have figured they were picking lint off a polecat's tail.

"You"—I poked one with my rifle muzzle—"move over to the other side."

When he had moved over I told him to rinse out a cup and fill it with coffee. Then I proceeded to eat a chunk of frying-pan bread and most of a frying pan of bacon, and to drink about half a gallon of coffee.

Meanwhile I'd looked this crowd over and had noticed a few things. This was no ordinary bunch of cowhands. They were mounted too well, their saddles were too good, and they were armed too well. I'd seen too many paid warriors in my time not to recognize these for what they were.

"You boys taken the wrong job," I said. "My advice is to light out. You ain't gonna like it here."

"Have your fun," one man said. "You ain't got long."

"None of us have. Only thing a body knows about life is that you're never going to get out of it alive. Only you boys don't want to wait for your time to come, you're asking me to bring it to you.

"Up to now I've been on the dodge. Now I'm going to start pot-hunting. I mean I'm going after scalps. Here and yonder I'm going to lay up and wait for you, and I'm going to shoot you when I see you. This here is all the warning you get."

Well, I backed off a mite and had one of them make a gather of pistol belts and rifles. It was likely some of them had hide-out guns, but I wasn't too worried about that. Then I had one of them saddle up my horse and pack my pack horse.

When I was up in the leather I sat there with my rifle over my saddle-bows and looked at them. "You ain't much," I said. "Why, when us Sacketts fought them Higginses back in the mountains we whopped them good...and any one of them would run you boys clean out of the county.

"Case you ain't been told the truth, your boss, or one of your bosses, murdered my wife when I left her alone in our wagon. Then he buried her body and burned my outfit. I figure some of you boys are complete coyote, and some are not. I'll know which is which by the ones who cut out and leave. No decent man would ride for a skunk like that."

"Who did it?" one of them asked.

"That I've got to find out. She scratched him up some when he fought her, but those scratches are likely healed by now. They are healed on the outside, but you can bet they scratched so deep he feels them yet, and somebody saw him while they were still raw."

"You've got the wrong idea," the man said. "The men who own the Lazy A are decent. You'd never find a better pair than Swandle and Allen."

"Maybe...but one of that pair is scared enough to pay you boys fighting wages to be rid of me. You figure that out for yourself."

"Why, you damn' fool! You ain't got a chance!"

"Maybe, but how many will I take along when I go? You ask yourselves that." I tapped my Winchester. "I can cut the buttons off your coat with this."

Then I reined my horse around and just rode on out of there, and nobody moved to stop me.

All those men back there were tough men. They had used guns and knew what a gun could do. They weren't taking any more chances than need be. None of them was hunting reputation, and they fought to win. They could sit quiet and listen to me because they felt their time would be coming, and there was no use risking death just to prove how brave they were.

Well, when I rode out of there I didn't waste any time. I headed south and moved right along, and when night fell I camped in Bearhide Canyon about a mile above the spring.

Truth of the matter was, they'd kept me so busy taking

care of my hide that I'd had no chance to hunt around to find the man responsible for Ange's death, but every time I tracked Lazy A cattle or riders, they seemed to come from a place over on Cherry Creek.

Could be I was wrong, but as I went along those tracks became many when I worked over in that direction. So, taking my time, I went on, working along the ridges under cover of the trees, easing myself in closer and closer, and all the while I saw more of the cattle wearing that brand.

There was the taste of anger in my mouth, the taste of a deep, abiding hate within me. I didn't like the feeling, but it was there, and these were days when the land where I rode had no law beyond what each man could deliver with his own hand.

Somewhere ahead of me a man waited, a man shaken by a terrible fear, a fear that sweated him at night and knotted his belly. It was not so much fear of me, as fear of what I might say. Already some would be looking askance at him, but not so many would have seen his clawed face...what had he done about that?

As long as I lived I would be a threat to him, as long as I lived he would not know when I might not suddenly appear to destroy all that he was or might have been. The man who molests a woman in the West is despised by all, and is hung as fast as ever they can get a rope on him. That man knew it. And all the time he knew deep in his gnawing guts that I was coming for him.

As I rode, I kept thinking of the man who had turned to look at Ange as he rode past us, leaving Globe. That might be the man.

So I rode my horse through the pines, hearing only the soft hoof-falls on the needles that cushioned the trail. Like a shadow we moved along the high ridges with the clouds close above. I rode him through the chill of morning and the damp of gathered fog. I carried my Winchester across my saddle, and the lead in its bullets were meant to find a place in his flesh, in his heart, at the source of his life's blood.

In the cool of a morning I came at last to Apache Ridge, and saw smoke rising from the valley beyond, so I rode down into Salt Lick Canyon and followed down the Tonto, and up through the breaks to Diamond Butte. Hunkered down on top of the butte, I studied what lay below, and within me my heart began to pound.

There were canvas-topped wagons there, and some tents, and a layout like an army camp, and there was a herd of horses watched by two riders.

Slow smoke was rising, and there was the distant clatter of pots, and the friendly movement and sounds of a cattle outfit on the move. Only this one had stopped, and with the fine grass they had found I did not wonder at it. This was a cattleman's heaven, but the man who had brought that herd here had, in one brief moment, turned his life into a hell.

Nobody had to tell me that this was a well-run outfit. A body could see it plain enough. The stock was in good shape, and so was all the gear I could lay eyes on. I studied that place, studied it and every move that was made down there.

There was a cook and his helper, there was a horse wrangler, and there was a man who sat with a rifle over his knees near the biggest of the three tents. He sat some distance away from a smaller tent, but facing it, and it was to that tent that I gave my attention. And all the time my mind was full of its dreadful thoughts.

Swandle and Allen...that was the name one of the men back there had said. These were the men who owned the Lazy A brand, and one of them anyway was the man I sought...the man who had killed my Ange, who had destroyed all that life meant to me.

We had come to this western country with hopes of our own place, a place where we could build, raise a family, and have the kind of home we'd never had. She had never had a real home at all, and I'd not had one since I was a youngster, and it was little enough I'd seen of my folks. There were

Sacketts scattered all over the country, but I'd seen none of them until I came down to Mora to see Ma and the boys. It had been a long spell...since before the war.

There was not one chance in a thousand that I would live beyond the death of the man I meant to kill. Not one chance that I could escape after the job was done, and at the moment I did not care.

Swandle and Allen...Swandle *or* Allen? I had to know which was the guilty man, and I had no idea how to find out, except that I had the feeling that when I found him I would know him.

I thought it was a wonder they had not posted a man up on this butte, for from here a body could watch the entire layout and see every move that was made. I hunkered down to wait, and I kept my rifle down so it would reflect no sunlight, nor was I wearing anything that would.

Of course, not many cowhands wore such truck on the range. Some of them had town outfits they wore to dances and the like. Most of them wore the best they could afford. I even had a broadcloth suit one time, myself.

The next thing they measured me for would probably be a wooden overcoat. But before they did that, I was going to get me a man.

Waiting up there on the butte, I got to thinking further on this thing that filled my mind. Up to now I'd been supposing whoever had done it had just happened on Ange there alone, but supposing it was that man we saw down in Globe, and he followed us?

Supposing, even, this wasn't the first woman he'd left dead behind him?

ELEVEN

About mid-morning four riders rode in from the west and dismounted. They stripped their gear from their horses and, leaving them to the wrangler, strolled over to the chuck wagon. One of the four was a man I recognized from Montana, where he had been riding for a cow outfit.

Al Zabrisky was a gunman, a warrior with a gun for hire. He was the sort of man a cow outfit hired when trouble was expected from jayhawkers, homesteaders, or herd-cutters, and he was good at his job.

He was tall, slightly stooped, and sour-looking. Sober, he was a shrewd and calculating enemy, but when drinking he was apt to go completely berserk. At such times he was mean, and a trouble-hunter. The other men were all strangers to me, but they were of much the same sort, the way I figured.

After a bit the wrangler returned with four fresh horses, all saddled up and ready for riding.

Just then the flap of the guarded tent was thrown back and that square-jawed man whom I'd talked to in O'Leary's saloon in Globe came out. He ignored Zabrisky and the others, but crossed over to where the man sat with the rifle across his knees. The guard stood up and they talked together.

All of a sudden, I began to feel uneasy. The two men looked all around, the guard pointed toward the far-off rim, but never once did they look toward Diamond Butte...and in another instant, I was moving.

When the notion took me I was squatting on my heels. I did not straighten up, but just turned on the balls of my feet and scooted into the brush behind me. Once hidden, I hesitated, taking time to listen, but there was no sound. Skirting the top of the butte, I came to the trail I'd made coming up. There I crouched among the rocks and waited.

It just didn't stand to reason that two men could look all around and ignore the biggest thing there was nearby. They had been discussing terrain, and if they ignored that butte it was because they had a reason for it. The only reason that came to mind was that they knew I was up there and they were fixing to surround me.

My horse was down below there, and they had found it. Flat out on my belly, I eased up behind a rock, then inched my head over to where I could look past it without outlining myself against the sky.

From where I lay I could see both my horses, but even as I located them a magpie swooped in for a landing in some brush near them. The magpie darted down, then suddenly swung sharply away. Somebody was hiding in that brush.

All right, so they knew where I was. My brain started to figure it out, and I knew they would have the butte surrounded. It was not so large but that a bunch of men could stake out every inch of it. So they had me.

But did they? What about the side where the camp was? It was dollars to doughnuts they never figured I would try that, and the chances were it was unguarded. There were men down there. There were horses, too, and saddles.

So I crawled around, looked the camp over for a minute or two, and then went over the edge. At that point the butte was not so steep, and there was cover here and there. I went down fast, running in short, quick spurts, keeping under cover when possible, crossing gaps as quickly as possible.

At the bottom of the slope I hunkered down behind a clump of brush and gave study to the lay-out before me. The four riders, including Zabrisky, had ridden off. The guard remained at his post, the wrangler was standing alongside the chuck wagon drinking coffee and talking to the cooks. The square-jawed man I'd seen in Globe had gone back into the tent. I now figured him for either Swandle or Allen.

Moving off to the right where my approach was covered

by a tent, I came out of the brush, my rifle hung to my hand and easy to use. I crossed behind the big tent and edged up behind the small one. Inside I could hear somebody scratching away with a pen.

Well, I taken a long chance. I wanted that man in there, and I wanted him bad. So I slung my Winchester to my shoulder and snaked out my Colt. I held the Colt in my right hand, and with my left I out with my bowie knife. Now, that big knife was honed like a razor—I'd shaved with it many a time—and I was counting on surprise. The last thing that man figured would be me right in the middle of his camp, so I stuck my knife into the back of the tent and slashed it wide with one quick sweep, and my Colt had that sitting man as its target. It had him, and it held him right like he was pinned.

"You could call out," I said, "but you don't size up like a man who'd want his last words to be yellin' for help."

He just sat there. At first, he just couldn't believe his eyes, but if he doubted them, he had no doubt at all about either that pistol or my intentions.

"I am not the man you want," he said.

"Maybe," I said. "If you are, I'll take you apart. Right now we're going to settle a little business.

"Some of your boys," I went on, "have my horse and pack outfit staked out over t'other side of the butte. I just naturally was of no mind to go fetch it, so I'll need a saddled horse, and a pack horse with four days' grub on it.

"You call that guard over here," I said, "and you tell him to have a horse saddled and a pack made up. Tell him to do it fast.

"Now, I know there's signals you could give that man, and I could be took...taken, I mean. I could be taken right here and now. But when they take me, they would take me with you dead at my feet. If you're the man I want, you know you'll die anyway, but if you ain't, you'd be an awful fool to die for what somebody else did."

"You're a fool, Sackett. Why don't you take the horse and ride out of the country? You haven't a chance."

"You order that horse. The only chance I want is to kill a man, the man who killed my Ange."

"I am sorry for that."

"Order the horse."

Well, he got up, very carefully, and he went to the tent flap. "Dancer? Saddle up that dun gelding, will you? Put Al's spare saddle on it. And a pack horse with a week's grub. I want it right away."

He came back and sat down. "You won't be likely to make it, but you'll get your chance. Take my advice and ride out of here."

"You don't look like a man who would murder a lone woman."

His face went white, and then he colored up. He was mad, clean through. "I know nothing about it...if it ever happened."

"It happened." Gesturing toward the tent flap, I said, "Your man Dancer was within a mighty close distance when it happened. He was among those who hunted me after Macon shot me off the cliff."

"You seem to be well informed."

"I overheard talk. They came mighty near me."

We stayed quiet a minute or two, but my ears were busy. The camp was going along just the way it had. No use my trying to watch outside, for I'd have to take my eyes off him. I would have to chance it, and mighty slim chance it was.

I shifted my Colt to my left hand and unslung my Winchester. Covering him with that, I thrust my Colt into my waistband. There was another gun lying there on the cot, so I picked it up.

"Whilst you're idle," I said, "you write out a bill of sale for that outfit I'm taking. Even swap for mine."

"You don't miss much, do you?" He wrote it out. "How can a man as shrewd as you buck such a stacked deck?"

"Mister, that girl of mine was all I had, all I ever had. She was murdered. I don't much care what happens to me as long as I get the man who did it. And I have an idea if a body did some hunting, he might find other dead women on that man's back trail."

His head swung around, his blue eyes hard. "What makes you say that?"

"I've read his sign, and it reads pure lobo. The man's a killer. At first I figured he went panicky, but now I ain't so sure. Maybe he was following a pattern he'd made up long since. There's folks missing out in this country, folks nobody will ever account for.

"This man is no youngster, that's how I read him. A man like that either knows better, or he's laid out his path long before."

We'd kept our voices low, and when the sound of the horses approaching became clear I held up a hand and he was still. The hoof-falls stopped outside the tent, and Dancer spoke.

"You ready, Mr. Swandle? I got the horses."

"Tell him to come in," I said.

"Come in, Dancer."

He came in, a solid, deep-chested cowpuncher with a shock of black hair and a broad, cheerful face. He looked at me, then at his boss. "Well, now. I was wonderin' why the pack hoss. You want I should try him?"

"No, Dancer. As you've probably guessed, this is Sackett."

Me, I put in my words. "Dancer, I've nothing against you. All I want is the name of the man who ordered you to hunt for me."

Dancer grinned right back at me. "Now you don't figure I'd tell you? You try to beat it out of me, and I'll whop you, big as you are. And ever'body for miles would know what was happenin'. Was I you, I'd give up right now."

"And have your boss hang me? He wants to do that, Dancer, and he wants you boys to help him. He wants his skirts clean on this."

"I want him to get out of this tent, Dancer," Swandle said. "I'll not lose a good man when I'm not sure what the stake is."

Me, I stood up, and had to bow my head to do it. "Dancer, I figure you're clear. I figure Swandle here is. I don't see fingernail marks on his face, and there weren't any when I saw him several weeks back. I saw Ange's nails before I buried her. She put up a fight...she was a little thing, but she fought, and she had hide and flesh under her nails."

A moment there I paused, listening. It sounded as if somebody was coming. "Dancer, you look like a man to ride the river with," I said, "so don't go to shooting for no man that would murder a lone woman."

His eyes studied my face, and then he stepped back out of the tent and held the flap. Motioning Swandle to go ahead, I followed them out.

It was still out there, a warm, lazy day of early spring. We could hear the voices at the chuck wagon.

"I'm going to ride clear. I'll tell you all just like I told the others...stay out of this. I'll kill any man who gets in my way."

"Everything I've got is in this outfit," Swandle said, "Every dime. If it's lost, then I'm broke."

"You figure what it's worth, mister. If they get me, there's fifty, maybe a hundred more Sacketts. They'll hear of it, and they will come ridin', as many as needed, and they'll keep comin' as long as they're needed. Maybe it don't make sense, Swandle. I ain't the one to say, but when somebody kills a Sackett he buys grief and death and disaster.

"You get shut of him or you'll go down with him, because I'll wipe him out. When I have to, I'll run; when I can, I'll fight, but whatever I do, I'll not quit. It ain't because I've got more nerve than the next man, it's just that I'm not very smart. Nobody ever taught me when was the time to quit."

I waved a hand around. "Mister, you get twelve dollars out of all you own, and you'll still be alive. You figure it. I never knew of a bullet that had any sense of discrimination.

I owe you no trouble, but you'll show up mighty black against a skyline."

"Do you want us to drop our belts?" Swandle asked.

"No...if shooting starts I never want it said I killed an unarmed man. You just stay clear."

With that, I taken my Winchester in hand and I led my horses over to the chuck wagon. I balanced the rifle easy-like and I said to the cook, "I'll have a gallon of coffee and that sandwich there. You like whiskey?"

"Hell, yes. What's that to do with it?"

"You fetch me that grub and you stand back, or you'll have so many holes in you, you'll drain whiskey faster'n you can drink it."

So I stood there and ate the beef and bread, swallowed the coffee, and then ate three-quarters of a fresh-baked apple pie, picking it up a quarter at a time and eating each quarter in three juicy bites. When I had wiped off my face with the back of my hand and had drunk the last of the coffee, I swung into the leather and looked around, sizing it all up.

"Mr. Swandle," I said, "Globe is a likely place. Why don't you boys ride off down thataway?"

That wrangler had been standing there, eyes bulging at me, and it was plain that something was worrying him. He was thinking of how when he told of this around the fire somebody might ask what he did, and so instead of being smart, he decided to have something to tell them.

He was wearing a belt gun and it was likely he had been doing some practice out back of the trees. Anyway, as I started to swing my horse, he grabbed iron.

He was a damned fool, for my rifle was gripped in my big right hand, and I'm tall and strong enough to use a rifle like a pistol, almost. So when he grabbed for it I tilted that Winchester and let him have it through the shoulder. It was no hard thing to do...he wasn't eighteen feet from me at the time.

He hit ground and stared up at me, hurt and sick-looking, because this was never the way he'd imagined it.

I said to him, "You go to pitchin' hay, son. You got the hands for it." And then I walked my horses away from there, knowing that rifle shot would bring them a-running.

Out of sight of camp, I lit out a-riding hard. Me, I had talked a big show, but I had no liking for forty men all to once. Or even half that many.

Back there I was counting on good sense, and most western men have it. They know that when a man holds a gun he more than likely is willing to use it, so there's no use to provoke him. That wrangler now, he'd live to get some sense. Most youngsters who want to pack a gun always see themselves winning. They never see themselves stretched out in the dirt and blood, with themselves shot open, and maybe crying from hurt and fear.

That night I camped in the cave under the natural bridge on Pine Creek, hard by Buckhead Mesa, and thought of Ange, lying cold in the ground not two miles off. I lay there awake into the small and lonely hours, a-thinking of her, and how little she'd had in her short years.

Nobody deserves to die like that, alone and in terror, hopeless with fear and pain. Had I not left her there, she might be alive now, but a dozen times before I'd gone ahead to scout trail, and a dozen times I'd hurried back to her side.

Tomorrow I was going to lay flowers on her grave. Tomorrow I would ride up Buckhead Mesa, and then I would ride to find my man.

A man named Allen....

TWELVE

On the ride to the cave I had taken mighty good care to keep under cover of the trees and brush. Studying the rim and the peaks round about, anywhere at all where a watcher might be, I worked to keep myself hidden. It was likely I'd gotten to the cave unseen, but there had been other times when I thought I was safe, and was not. But the way up Pine Creek through the canyon was so hidden that a watcher would have had to ride right on my tail to see me at all.

If Allen was my man he had little time now. He knew as well as I that time was a-pressing.

This much I'll say for Swandle. He had given me a mighty fine horse in trade, and with the bill of sale I had for it and for the pack horse, he would never get me on horse-stealing.

Al Zabrisky I had seen, but where were Romero, Sonora Macon, and the others? It took me no time at all to find out.

Before daylight I was out of the cave and moving. Along the way I gathered some spring flowers and put them on Ange's grave. Then I turned back to my horse and saw three riders coming up through the trees.

There was no chance to run, nor was I of a mind to. If they wanted it, they could have it. So right there I made my stand, in the open and with my Winchester to hand.

They didn't see me right off. They came riding up, coming out of the trees maybe thirty yards off, all of them riding Lazy A horses.

"You hunting me?" I yelled at them.

They pulled up short. One of them grabbed for his gun and I shot him out of the saddle. Then I dropped to one knee and fired again, jacked another shell into the chamber, and was firing my third shot before the first one came in reply. It was a clean miss. The rider I'd got with my first shot was on the ground. His horse had shied as he fell, disturbing the aim of the others. I fired again and the two remaining riders lit out for the brush on a dead run, one of them hanging to the saddle horn with his left hand, his right dangling useless.

Keeping the fallen man covered, I walked up to him. He was hurt bad, shot through the chest. He was a big, bearded man with a scar on his face, and he stared up at me, fully conscious.

"Am I going to die?"

"You came hunting me. What d'you expect?"

Picking up his guns, I studied him for hide-outs, and then I walked over to where his horse had stopped. I took his Winchester and his saddlebags, although what they contained I had no idea.

"He'll get you," the wounded man said. "Allen will get you."

When I did not answer, he said, "You ain't got a chance. This time he's got a plan."

"What plan?"

"You're already trapped. You couldn't leave this country if you wanted. They've got you surrounded and now they're going to move in."

"He hasn't got that many men."

His face was white and he was sweating with the pain he was beginning to feel as the shock wore off. "He's got maybe a hundred Apaches....He's promised 'em...rifles and whiskey." The words came with difficulty.

Apaches...

That would do it, all right. The White Mountain or Tonto Apaches would know this place inside and out. This was their country, and they would know every nook and cranny. The circle would tighten and tighten, with me in the middle. I'd seen wolves hunted on the prairie in just that way.

The man died while I stood there looking down at him.

I mounted up and rode out of there. I headed due west, riding hard and steady. I held to low ground, and saw nobody. Twice I did see signal smokes in the distance, a sure sign that what the man had said about the Apaches was true.

This was rugged, broken country, and what I needed now was speed. At Dead Cow Canyon I turned south and plunged into the lonely wilderness of the Mazatzal Mountains.

It was hot and still. The coolness of the morning was far behind me now, and the climbing had worked my horses hard. On the slope of a cactus-covered ridge I drew up to let them breathe and to contemplate the countryside.

It was good to sit quiet a moment and look upon the land, for the flowers were out and it was carpeted with beauty. Little enough time I had for that, but it came to me through the air I breathed, for the loveliness of this land was always with one who traveled through it.

Far away the mountains were a blue rim. Close by, the canyons clung to their shadows, and setting quiet up there, I just let my eyes roam over the far country and the near, watching, searching.

The Apache of the mountains is a fierce man, given to fighting and raiding, a man who knows his way about, and is always near when he seems far away. The numbers were so against me that there were only two things I could do...I could find some place to hole up, leaving no tracks and hoping they would not find me; or I could try to filter through, to work my way into the outside and then ride for an Army post or Globe or Prescott and wait until Allen tired of paying Apaches. But my chances of getting through were slim indeed, and of hiding places there was no chance I could find one that was not already known to the Apaches.

Far away a slim column of smoke lifted, and nearer I could see a small puff of dust, so I walked my horses up the slope and crossed Cactus Ridge on a low saddle and pointed north, toward Knob Mountain.

I thought back to Swandle. He had been stern, but almost

friendly. I could believe that he did not approve of what Allen was doing—Allen, the man who remained a mystery to me. And suddenly I remembered the startled look on Swandle's face when I mentioned there might have been other women like Ange. Almost as if he knew something of the sort.

But it was time to face the facts. It was I, not he, who was being hunted by a superior force, and my chance of escape, let alone the chance of facing the guilty man, were almighty small. I was alone, and the forces moving against me were more than I could hope to defeat, and still I had not even seen the man I searched for, nor did I know anything about him beyond the mere name.

Never in my life before had I wished for help, but I found myself wanting it now. I realized that there was almost no chance of my doing the hunting. Somewhere I had to find a place to hide out.

Coming off the shoulder of Knob Mountain, riding toward Midnight Mesa, I saw three riders ahead of me. They came out of the trees and were riding down toward me. Rifle across my saddle, I rode toward them.

They spread out a little when they saw me, but I kept right on, seeming to pay them no mind. My mouth was dry, and I was wary, because no man likes to tackle three tough men head-on, and any man I'd meet riding for Lazy A would be a tough man now. But on the steep slope there was no chance to run. It was bluff or fight, and so I kept right on.

As they drew up, all three were set for trouble, and then I saw one of them glance at the brand on my horse...I'd forgotten it was a Lazy A horse.

He chuckled. "Had me worried there for a minute or two," he said. "I thought you was Sackett."

They had all relaxed when they saw my brand, but I kept that rifle on them. "I am Sackett," I said. "You boys unbuckle. And if you want to lose your hair, just have at it."

Oh, they were mad, no question about it, and they dearly wanted to try for their guns, but they had ridden too many trails to want to die easy. They used their fingers mighty careful as they unbuckled.

Then I backed them off about thirty yards and made them dismount. I taken their horses and collected their guns. There was a pack of grub on one of the horses, and I tossed it to them.

"Eat," I said, "and then walk down to the Verde. Sooner or later somebody will come along, or you can high-tail it up to Camp Verde."

Two of them had cartridges I could use, so I stripped the loops of their gun belts. Their six-shooters I hung on a tree where they could be seen, but their rifles I kept. No telling when I might have to fight and no chance to re-load.

And then I rode off and left them cussing me, which I didn't mind, nor did I blame them. It was a sore thing to be set afoot in rough mountain country, with riding boots and a long walk ahead of you.

That night I hid out in the breaks back of Wet Bottom Creek—named for a cowpuncher who fell in—and I cooked myself a batch of bacon and some frying-pan bread. Their horses I had turned loose near sundown, figuring they would head back for the ranch.

Just short of daybreak I rolled out of my blankets and was putting my outfit together for the trail when I heard a quail call. Something about it didn't seem right to me. There were quail all over this country, the blue Mexican quail, but that call sounded a mite odd. So I saddled up and packed up fast.

Meanwhile, another quail answered, and then a third.

My camp had been on an almost level spot under the cottonwoods and sycamores beside the creek. It was a quiet, pleasant place, with the creek chuckling along over the stones, and when the sun was up the ground under the trees was dappled with sunlight and shadow.

Below me the canyon's walls rose almost sheer, and the canyon bottom was rarely touched by sunlight. At the point where I had made camp there was an open space, all of a half-mile long and perhaps a third as wide, with good grass. It was on the edge of this open area that I'd made my camp.

It looked across the stream toward the north and toward a canyon that opened out from that direction. On my right the upper canyon of Wet Bottom led back up toward Bull Spring Canyon and an ancient Indian trail.

It was a likely place, and I'd had hopes of staying a while, letting my horses rest and getting some rest for myself. After the bad fall I'd had I hadn't yet fully regained my strength although I was much better. Now they had found me—of that I had no doubt. The question was, could I get out and away?

Down canyon might be the safest. Nobody was going to chase me down there, not if they were in their right mind. One man with a rifle could hold off an army there. But once out of the lower canyon I was in the valley of the Verde, and I could lay money there would be Lazy A riders or Indians patrolling along the river.

Those quail calls were likely to be Apaches, and I could expect nothing but trouble from them. The fact that some of them had helped me before meant nothing now, for the chances were slight that they would be the same bunch. Even if they were, they would be ready to earn the rewards offered them.

It was very still. Taking the bridle and lead rope, I walked to the far side of the clearing, listened, then stepped into the water of the stream. The bottom here was flat rock and coarse gravel, the water clear and cold. It had been a wet spring in this stream, which occasionally almost disappeared, was now running eighteen inches to two feet deep. As the water started to deepen, I stepped into the saddle.

The shoulder of the mesa was close on my right, and I thrust my rifle into its scabbard to give myself greater freedom of movement. Any action now would be pistol action, for a man could see only a few yards in any direction.

Overhead a buzzard swung in lazy, expectant circles. The horses made little sound as they walked through the water, and I could see nothing, wherever I looked. Used as I was to being alone, I found a longing in me for somebody to help me watch out... I was up against too much, and unless I had more luck than I could expect, my time was short.

A flash of sunlight on a rifle barrel warned me, and I ducked and jumped my horse with a touch of the spur. I heard the wicked slap of a bullet against the rock wall, and then the echo ringing along the canyon. Almost without willing it, my eyes had turned toward where the shot struck, and I saw a white scar on the face of the rock, not over four feet above the water, so whoever had shot was up on the mountain opposite.

Just as I was searching for the spot from which he'd fired, he raised up to shoot again. It was a far piece for a pistol, so I simply held my fire and pushed my horses toward the shoulder of the rock. As I did so, an Indian suddenly showed on the bank of the stream not twenty feet off.

The soft echoes of my splashing had misled him as to where I was, and he came out of the brush with his eyes pointing about twenty feet behind me, and by the time he could swing them into focus it was too late. I shot across my body at him, and saw the bullet drill his chest. He raised up to his tiptoes, then fell splash into the water. And then I was around the corner and going up Wet Bottom as fast as I could make it.

When I reached the trail crossing at Bull Spring Canyon I turned left and went up the canyon with both horses going all out. About a hundred yards up I slowed down, not wanting to kill the horses, and when I reached the top of the mesa the trail branched. I'd been waiting for that, figuring they might have a man at Bull Spring where the trail split.

They had one there, all right. They had three. I'd been walking my horse, and we made no sound on the deep pine needles along there. Just as I sighted them I gave him a touch of the spur and went into the three of them as if I'd been shot from a gun.

My horse staggered, but he kept his feet, but one of theirs

went down, and I shot point-blank into one of the men. I felt a bullet burn my shoulder and almost dropped my gun ...almost.

We swung right, ducked into the rocks and legged it for the rim of the canyon, which gave me shelter just in time to hear a couple of bullets going overhead. That burn was more than a surface burn, because I could feel blood inside my shirt, and I swore like an Irish gandy-dancer at the knowledge that they'd winged me again.

Then other shots rang out and I felt my horse going under me, and I jumped free just in time. I could hear hoofs pounding the trail from both directions, and I had only time to grab my rifle and hit the rocks before they came sweeping around the bend.

Well, they ran into trouble.

There I was, belly down in the tall grass and rocks, with cactus to left and right of me, and a good Winchester. I poured it to them. They had come asking for it and I shot as fast as I could throw them, and then I grabbed my six-shooter and dusted them off with that.

They broke and ran, with one man down and a horse running free, and another man swearing a blue streak and hanging to his saddle-horn with both hands. His back was bloody. That fellow down on the sand wasn't even twitching.

In the moment I had, I made a dive for that horse. I came out with three rifles and belts. I picked up, and I sprinted for deeper cover among the rocks and felt the whip of a bullet past my face.

Well, those boys wanted me, and they were being paid fighting wages. If they were going to be paid for it, they might as well earn it.

I settled down and studied the land. They could come at me from two ways, and either way was going to be mighty uncomfortable.

Oh, they had me, all right. They had me up the creek without a paddle, but when they salted my hide I'd have plenty of company.

They couldn't come at me very easy, but I had an idea they'd try to get on the canyon wall above me. Come night-time, I was going to have to squeeze out of there, somehow or other.

An hour passed, and then another. The sun was hot and I was glad that soon I was going to be on the shadowed side of that cliff. But when it became dark I wasn't going to be able to see them closing in, so they were in no hurry.

Nobody moved...a cicada sang in the brush...that buzzard was keeping track of me, for I saw his shadow as he swept overhead. I checked my rifles, reloaded the shells I'd fired, then checked my six-shooter.

The furrow that had been laid in my shoulder was shallow, and it had stopped bleeding. My mouth was dry and I wished for a drink, but my canteen was back there on my horse. The thought came to me of a sudden that I might never get another drink of water. They really had me pinned down now, right back up against Bullfrog Ridge, with the river facing me but a good half-mile or more away.

Suddenly a bullet hit the rock above me, whipping by my head with a nasty whine. And then I was really scared.

This was a trick the soldiers had used on the Apaches in the cave not far from here. They couldn't get at the Indians, so they shot against the back wall...ricochets can tear a man up something awful, and I had talked to men who saw what was in that cave afterwards.

I hunted myself a hole, found a narrow crack in the rocks, and squeezed in.

For the next half-hour there was lead and rock chips flying every which way, and if they had come with a rush then they'd have had me sure. I couldn't have gotten out in time to stand them off, but they didn't know that.

Dust got in my eyes, and several times I was stung by chips of flying rock, but no bullet reached me. The way I was squeezed in there, it would have been a miracle if I had been shot, and after a while they gave up. I scrambled out of the hole, and studied the place down there toward the river bank where they'd been shooting from. Seeing nothing of them, I fired a shot to show them I was still around.

Twilight came, and in the desert country there is mighty little of that. Stars started to show up, and I hunted a place to hide. This was going to be the showdown, I could feel it in my bones. They had me treed, and there was just no way out. Judging by the shooting, there'd been a dozen or more men down there. I thought of my horses—the horse I rode was down, and the pack horse had run off a little way, but he might as well have been ten miles off.

The desert air was clear and I could hear the men talking as the night drew on. I could smell the smoke of their fire, and thought I could even smell bacon frying and coffee. It made my stomach growl, for I'd eaten nothing since the night before.

The more I thought of that grub the more I wanted some. They had me, all right, but I might as well die with a full stomach. Maybe I should go down there, Injun up on them and walk in shooting. I'd get a full stomach all right...full of lead.

Just after full dark a rider came in. I heard their greetings. Heard him say "...one hell of a fight. I don't know where those two came from, but when they were called on they delivered."

"Where was it?"

"Solomonville. Dodie Allen went into this place with Pete Ryland and Collins. They weren't hunting trouble, but you know how Dodie is. Just because his uncle's a big cattleman, he thinks he is too. Or he thought he was."

"Dead?"

"You ain't a-woofin'. Why, he no more'n picked trouble with those two than he was dead."

"What started it?"

"Dodie. He started it. He had two tough men with him, and I guess he figured he was safe. Or maybe he figured he'd been growin' more hair on his chest. Anyway, he said those two looked like they come right out of the hills.

"One of them fellers, he just looked over at him an' said, 'Mebbe.'

"Then Dodie said this here was a rough country on folks from Tennessee—that they had one cornered up in the hills, and they were going to stretch rope with his neck come daylight.

"This here tallest one, he said, 'You-all huntin' a man name of Sackett?' And Dodie, he said he sure was. Collins, he was nudgin' Dodie to shut up, but you know that kid. He's bull-headed as an ornery calf. Dodie said he sure was, and this feller just pulled back an' said, 'You found yourselves two of 'em. You goin' to draw that gun, or suck aigs?'

"Well, sir, Dodie he didn't know what to do. All of a sudden his loud mouth had talked him right into it, and he showed what he was made of. He just stood there swallowin' air and turnin' greener by the minute.

"Ryland, he cut in and said Dodie meant nothin' by it, but they wouldn't let him be.

"'He said you-all was huntin' Sacketts,' the tall one said. 'Well, you found two. I'm Flagan Sackett, and this here's Galloway. You goin' to start shootin', or runnin'?' So they started shootin'."

"Dead?"

"All three of them...four shots fired. Four shots killed those boys. Dodie took two of them."

There was silence, and then some murmuring talk I couldn't hear, and then somebody said, "What'll the boss say about that? He set store by Dodie."

"He's fit to be tied. You know how Van is. He's got a temper and he really flew off the handle when he heard it. And Skeeter, too."

"I wouldn't want to be those Sacketts when Skeeter Allen catches up with them."

"I wouldn't want to be Skeeter. You never saw them two work."

It was quiet for a few minutes, and then a voice said, "How about some of that coffee?"

It was time to start moving if I was ever going to try getting out of there. All the shells I had, I loaded in my pockets or the loops of my cartridge belt. Another beltful I slung across my shoulder like a bandolier. Then I took my own rifle and a spare, and eased down among the rocks.

My mind was a-puzzling over those two Sacketts. There weren't any Sacketts closer than Mora, over in New Mexico, or none that I knew of. It came to mind, though, that there had been a man named Flagan Sackett who lived over at Denney's Gap. This here might be a grandson, or some other relation.

If that tale I'd just heard was true, they sure sounded like Sacketts to me. It was a comfort to feel that maybe I wasn't all alone after all.

Well, I sort of seeped down through those rocks onto the flat land near the river. Those boys had them a big fire, and it threw a lot of light around. If they had been talking around that fire for long they wouldn't be able to see good in the dark, and...

All at once an Indian came up off the ground right at my feet. My eyes took the flash of light against a knife blade and I shot my rifle as if it was a pistol, jamming the muzzle against the body and squeezing her off.

As the Indian went down, I lifted the rifle to my shoulder and emptied it into the crowd around the fire, and you never saw such a scattering. A horse dashed near me, and I dropped the empty rifle and grabbed at him.

I laid hold, but he jerked me off my feet and I hit ground, luckily hanging onto my rifle. Bullets were dusting sand all about me and I made a scramble for the rocks. And so there I was, fairly trapped again.

Well, I'd dealt them some misery. They would have that to remember. I crawled back into the rocks, working my way back toward the cliff.

Van Allen...for the first time I had the name of the man I wanted, but where was he, and how could I get to him? I laid up there in the rocks, hungry as all get-out, parched for a drink, trying to figure a way out. If it was going to happen, it would have to be at night. When daylight came they were sure as shootin' going to get me. But give me a horse and I'd light out as if the heel flies were after me.

All of a sudden a fire sprang up…I could hear the dry branches crackling clear back where I was. The fire was off to my left a little. Then another one came alive off to my right. First thing I knew they had five fires going down there, and it lit up the shore of the Verde all the way along in front of me. Somewhere behind those fires were men with rifles, and beyond them the horses I'd need.

It began to look as if they had me now.

THIRTEEN

It was a bitter end that faced me, surrounded by enemies and my back to the wall, but it was not death I was thinking of, but only that I'd let the man live who had killed Ange. She whom life had given so little, to be murdered at the end of it and thrown aside like a used-up thing.

Somewhere out there was Van Allen, always safely out of danger's way, always in the background so that I'd not even know his face if we met. The fires out there were lighting the only way I had of escape, unless I could scale the cliffs behind me. But their light touched upon the cliff too, and I did not wish to pin myself against a wall as a target for their rifles.

Well, if their story was true, there were other Sacketts in the country, and it would not end with me. Where my body lay, others would lie, for Van Allen had no idea when he followed us from Globe that day what hell he was inviting.

A faint stirring in the night warned me, and I moved from where I was. They were creeping up along the cliff, creeping through the rocks to meet me. It would not be a rifle's work when they came close, but work for a pistol.

Then I thought of a long-dead branch I'd seen among the rocks, and I felt for it. Carefully I lifted it up, and stirred the brush eight or ten feet from where I waited. After a moment, I dragged it ever so lightly along the leaves, hoping they would hear it.

Hear they must have, for suddenly they closed in with a rush on the spot just in front of me, and I think it was in their minds to have me alive. I emptied my Colt with one continuous sound like a roll of thunder, then slipped off to one side, grasping my rifle and crouching low. Gun fire stabbed the night, and laced a criss-cross above my head and over to the side where I had been. Putting my rifle down, I thumbed shells into my gun again...six of them, and waited.

There was a thrashing around in the brush, and a man cried out in pain. Somebody else was moaning—terrible, shuddering moans. Well, they had asked for it.

Ever so carefully, I eased back from where I was, going around a boulder, and then my boot came down on a dry branch. In an instant the night was whipped by streaking fire. Something slugged me in the wind, and I felt my knees buckle, and I shot and shot again.

Falling, I went down on a man, his face slippery with blood. Gasping for breath and clutching my empty pistol, I ran my hand out along his arm to his hand and twisted the gun free. He was beyond resisting.

In the darkness I crouched there, feeling the slow sickness of a wound coming over me. I put the captured gun down and reloaded the other and leathered it. Rifle in one hand, six-gun in the other, I backed away from the man...dead or fatally wounded, I did not know which.

My breath was coming in rasping gasps now. Whether I was shot through the lung or was merely gasping from the effort of movement I had no idea.

From out on the bottom land someone called out, "Well, what happened?"

Somebody moaned, but there was no other reply. Anybody who was alive wasn't about to make a target of himself by speaking.

I dragged myself back further, feeling sick and empty, and my head humming with hurt. I couldn't understand why I felt as I did.

Men appeared between me and the light—three of them. It took a mighty effort to get the rifle around, but I made it. They were coming closer...I guess they thought everybody was dead. So I fired, and dropped the one who lagged. I did not think I had killed him, for his leg buckled, but the others ran left and right but not quickly enough that I did not nail another one. I heard him yelp, and he dived away into the darkness.

And then for a time all was still. Maybe I passed out, I do not know. Only when my eyes opened I was looking to the stars and it was quiet all around me. The fires still flared, but nobody moved that I could hear. I lay there in pain, and felt terribly alone. There was no will in me to move...only a wishing to hear the wild turkeys calling on the Big South Fork, or to smell the dogwood in April above Crab Orchard.

The night smelled of pine and blood, and there was a wafting of wood smoke from the fires that lighted my way to dying. Only somehow I knew then I was not going to die until I had killed Van Allen. Until I had faced that shadowy figure, that somebody out there whom I had never seen, but who had struck down the girl I loved.

It was a feeling of foolishness that came over me that finally made me move, a realization that no man as tall and tough as I was had a right to die with such melancholy on him.

So I moved, and endured the swift pain that followed, and the sickness. I'd been hit in the side, I thought, when scarce beyond the knock on my skull from Sonora Macon's bullet, and the hurts of my fall.

There was another one I owed...Sonora Macon. Where was *he?*

My enemies all seemed beyond me, out of my reach, and even with me running so hard and so long, I could not come upon them.

The fires burned bright out there. No doubt their light was reflected from the face of these rocks where I lay, and a movement here could be seen. Perhaps some of them still lay living among the rocks, waiting for me to move, so they could kill me.

But I knew that somehow I had to live long enough to meet Allen, somehow this must be done. It was the knowledge that other Sacketts might come that helped me then...that they might even be close by.

I was a man who had always stood alone, aware of my family though far from it, aware of their instinct for pride of family and their readiness to die for it. No matter that it made little sense to some…a man must have something in which to believe, and with us who were Tennessee Sacketts the family came first. Everything—life, food, shelter—all came after.

For a hundred years my family had told stories of Sacketts who came running to help Sacketts, often men they had never known. It was the way of our kind, the way of the hills in which we were bred.

The place where I now crouched among the rocks was only a few miles from where Ange had been killed…maybe five or six miles. Buckhead Mesa was almost due north.

There were steep canyons to the right and left of the cliff, canyons that allowed water to fall off the mesa in quick cataracts…when there was water to fall. I did not know if I could climb, but I must try, for in the morning they would come at me. If I was going to make a stand I'd have to get well up among the higher rocks, above the bottom land.

Inch by inch, I began to work my way back and up. There were cracks in the rock, and there were clumps of brush, a few small steep slopes, and some ledges. My side hurt me, and my head ached heavily. I could scarce pull up my own weight, but I made it up a few feet, waited a bit, then edged on. Certainly no Apaches were close by, or they'd have heard me.

Once I'd started, there was brush enough on the slope to give me a little cover, but it was steep and I needed special care to keep my rifle from hitting against a rock, for the sound would be heard by any watchers below.

In the reflected light against the wall, I could see a little space beyond a juniper that grew out from the rock. Pushing past it, not without some noise, I found a space not over three feet wide, but it evidently ran along the cliff for some distance. Here was a layer of sandstone that had remained when softer rock had been eroded away—there were many such places in these hills. It gave me a place to rest, and some cover from the men down below.

I had panted and struggled, I had tugged and hauled my way up the side of the mountain, and now that I'd found even this small shelter, I just hadn't anything to go on with. The bitter hard days of riding, my wounds, and the exhaustion suddenly closed in on me. I lay down and the darkness closed around me. The night was fresh and the stars clear, and I slept.

A shout awakened me. I came out of the darkness of sleep...I came out a-clawing and a-grabbing, and then I sat up, soaked in cold sweat. It was full daylight, and there were men down below, among the rocks where I'd been.

They were that close, and they were hunting for me. I started to get up, but I couldn't make it. My legs were too weak to hold me, and I just sat down again there where I'd been. By leaning a mite I could see them...there were maybe twenty of them down there. I could see their horses back toward the river, in the bottom land. They were held in a rope corral by a wrangler.

Reaching out, I fumbled a grip on my Winchester and drew it to me.

"All right," I said, "you got me. But you're gonna pay to collect." I said it to myself as I eased the Winchester up where I could use it.

And then I heard a rattle among the rocks above me, and a pebble bounced down, struck my shoulder, and fell away among the rocks. A little dust trailed after.

So they were up there too. They were above me as well as below. This time they figured to make it a certain thing.

FOURTEEN

B ob O'Leary looked through the glass he was polishing, then added it to the stack on the back bar. He was worried and scared, and he was anxious for the night to end. Nobody was talking, although the saloon was half full.

Al Zabrisky was there, seated at a table in a corner with Burns and Briscoe. O'Leary knew them all, and not favorably, from Mobeetie and Tascosa. He wanted them to leave, but was far too wise a man to order them out. Zabrisky was drinking, and O'Leary knew what that meant, though as yet he had not had much.

Swandle was at the bar, standing alone. He looked thinner, older, and tired. O'Leary knew part of the story and could guess the rest. Swandle had every cent he owned invested in cattle in partnership with Van Allen, and those cattle had just finished a long desert drive a few weeks before. They had lost cattle on that drive and the stock needed time on the lush Tonto grass to recuperate. Swandle wanted no part of the fight Allen had brought on them, but he was unable to get out without losing everything.

O'Leary had just picked up another glass when the door opened. He looked that way and felt something freeze up tight within him. At first glance he thought the newcomer was Tell Sackett, but this man was heavier. He wore his hair down to his shoulders, and there was a scar on his cheekbone.

He wore two tied-down guns and his fringed buckskin jacket was open, showing the butt of a third. He was dusty and unkempt, and he paused momentarily in the door to let his eyes grow accustomed to the light. His nose had been broken in more than one fight, and there was a wild, reckless look about him that made O'Leary's heart miss a beat. He came on to the bar, spurs jingling, a powerful big man with the movements of a stalking lion.

"Rye," he said, then let his eyes drift over the room. They found Zabrisky and rested there, then examined both Burns and Briscoe.

Briscoe, who was the youngest of the three, saw him first, and spoke in an undertone to the others. Zabrisky turned his eyes toward the bar.

Nolan Sackett looked down the room at him and said, "Folks down the trail said somebody up here was huntin' a Sackett."

"So?" It was Zabrisky who spoke.

"I'm Nolan Sackett, of the Clinch Mountain Sacketts, and I've come a fur piece jus' to he'p my kinfolk."

Al Zabrisky had not yet had too much to drink, but what he'd had was working on him. What sanity remained warned him that he was drawing fighting wages to kill *Tell* Sackett. Furthermore, there was nothing about this big, uncurried wolf that appealed to him. The name Nolan Sackett had rung a bell...it was a name known wherever outlaws congregated, from Miles City to Durango in Mexico.

The word that came over the grapevine was loud and clear: *Nolan Sackett? Leave him alone.*

"We're not huntin' you," he said.

"Mister, you're huntin' a Sackett, an' the one you're huntin' would, man to man, make you eat that six-gun you're packin'. Howsoever, when you hunt one Sackett, you just naturally make the rest of us feel the urge.

"Now, I don't know if I'll make it up there in time to he'p, so I figured to trim off the edges, like. You look maverick to me, so I figured to put the Sackett brand on you."

There were five other Lazy A gun-handlers in the room. Swandle was at the bar, almost in the line of fire.

For the first time in his life, Al Zabrisky was prepared to talk himself out of a hole. He was a moneyfighter, and there was nothing in this but trouble with a capital T. He started to speak, but his gun holster was in his lap, the butt within easy inches of his hand. Suddenly he thought, *The hell with it!* And he grabbed the bone handle of his six-shooter.

Zabrisky's eye was quick and accurate, but he never saw the draw that killed him. He saw Sackett's hand move and then he was blinded by a stabbing light from the gun muzzle and the wicked blow of a .45 slug taking him in the stomach.

"What...?" He wanted to know what was happening to him, but only the dead could have told him. He started to go down, heard the stabbing roar of guns, and clawed his fingers into the boards of the saloon floor.

Burns was down. In a hurried move backward, his chair had tipped, and when he came up he caught a bullet over the right eye.

At the moment of drawing, Briscoe had thrown himself aside, getting out of the line of fire, but in so doing he lost his grip on his gun. It lay on the floor, inches from his hand. He looked at the gun, then at Nolan Sackett, who stood with his big feet apart, the six-shooter easy in his fist.

"Go ahead, son," Nolan said mildly, "go right ahead an' pick it up. Nobody gets to live forever."

Briscoe was sweating. The gun was close. He could grasp, tilt, and fire. He had a hunch he could do it and kill Nolan Sackett. His ambition told him to go ahead and grab, but his body had better sense, and his muscles refused to respond. Slowly, he sagged back.

Nolan Sackett took a quick step forward. "Here, boy. You might as well have it." He tossed the gun to Briscoe, and the gunman leaped back as if it were red-hot, letting the pistol fall to the floor.

Nolan Sackett shook his head reprovingly. "Son, you take it from me. Don't never tie one of those on again. Somebody will feed it to you."

He turned back to the bar and was startled to see a tall elegant young man in a tailored broadcloth suit, a black planter's hat, and Spanish-made boots holding a gun on another table of riders.

The gun was beautifully made, inlaid with gold, and it had pearl grips. Its mate was in its holster, butt forward, on the stranger's left side.

Without averting his eyes from the men at the table, the stranger said, "How are you, Nolan? I am Parmalee Sackett, from under the Highland Rim."

"A flat-land Sackett? I heard tell of 'em. Never did meet up with one before."

"These lads were getting a bit restless," Parmalee Sackett said. "It seemed a good idea to restrain them."

He holstered his pistol. "I'll buy a drink, Nolan, and if these boys gets fractious, we'll share and share alike."

"Only if you let us in," came a voice from the doorway. They turned to face the newcomers.

Orlando Sackett and the Tinker, newly arrived in Globe, walked across to the bar, and were greeted.

Parmalee Sackett turned to Swandle. "I understand you are one of the owners of the Lazy A?"

Swandle straightened up. "I am not wearing a gun."

"This isn't gun trouble," Parmalee replied. "This is business. How much of an outfit do you have?"

"We drove in three thousand head, or a mite over. We lost cattle on the drive."

"You want to sell out?"

"What?" Swandle stared at him. "Sell out to *you*?"

"Why not? You've got everything tied up in that herd, or so they told me. They also told me they doubted if you had anything to do with this trouble."

"I didn't. I'll take an oath. This was Allen's doing."

"All right, I'll buy you out, lock, stock, and barrel."

"You'd become a partner of Allen's?"

"That's right."

"Look," Swandle protested, "the cattle are scattered. Nobody has tried to do a thing with them since this trouble started. The remuda is worn to a frazzle, chasing this kin of yours, and Allen won't listen to anyone. He's obsessed...or scared to death."

"The way it looks to me you can stay in and take a gamble on losing it all, or you can sell out now."

"I bought cheap and I'll sell cheap. We picked our cattle up in Chihuahua for little or nothing."

"Name your best price."

Swandle hesitated, but he knew he was going to accept. A few hours before, he had been debating the question of riding out and just leaving it all behind. In fact, he had been thinking that way for several days past. Now he had his chance to ride out with enough to start elsewhere.

What was the real truth of the matter he did not know. He only knew that Tell Sackett's story had sounded convincing, and that Allen had been acting very queer. He also knew that most of the old hands, the hands hired in Texas, had gone. The ones who remained were hired gun hands or no-account drifters.

He had tried reasoning with Allen, but the man would not listen. He had offered to give Allen a note for his, Allen's, share of the cattle and outfit, but Allen had refused to either sell or buy.

Swandle's reputation was good. This he knew, and he knew that in the West even more than elsewhere business was done on reputation.

Now he named his price, and it was low. It was low enough so Parmalee Sackett would not back out, even if he were so inclined. "You've no idea what you're getting into," Swandle warned. "Van Allen is a dangerous man, and he's half-crazy now. All he can think of is killing Tell Sackett."

"If he hasn't killed him by now, he won't."

Parmalee Sackett took a letter from his pocket. "Do you know Fitch and Churchill, the Prescott attorneys?"

"I've done business with them."

"They represent me. Their offices are over the Bank of Arizona, and there is money enough on deposit there to cover this. Take this over to Tom Fitch or Clark Churchill—and you can write me out a bill of sale now."

Swandle stood at the bar and asked for a sheet of paper.

When Parmalee Sackett had glanced over the bill of sale, he turned on the Lazy A riders.

"You have heard us make a deal. I am now an equal partner in the Lazy A, and as of now, you are fired. As I understand it, you were hired without the knowledge of Mr. Swandle for a purpose having nothing to do with handling cattle. Therefore, if you are to be paid, you can collect from Mr. Allen...or you can go into court and sue me."

Slowly, the men got up. They did not like what they had heard, and liked still less this stranger dude. He had covered them without warning, without their even being aware of his presence, and now he had fired them.

"We got other ways of collecting," one of them said.

Parmalee Sackett nodded. "Of course. You are wearing a gun, so how about now?"

Barney Mifflin, faced with the situation, decided he did not care for it. There was a good chance he would collect nothing for all the riding and shooting he had already done, and only minutes before he had had a demonstration of the brand of shooting at least one Sackett could deliver.

"How about him?" Barney indicated Nolan.

"If it is going to be one at a time, he's out of it. Come on, gentlemen, the line forms on the right. Put up or shut up."

Barney hesitated, then shrugged. "The stakes are too high for what's in the pot. We'll ride out."

Deliberately, Parmalee turned his back to them. But Barney, an observant young man, noticed that he watched them in the mirror.

Outside in the street he said, "I wished I was riding for them. That's an *outfit*."

"Hell!" one of the others said, and he spat into the dust. "They don't need any help. Just the same," he added, "I'd like to be a little bird a-settin' in a tree when the show does come off."

Parmalee turned to the bar. "Nolan, how about that drink?" Then he looked at Orlando and the Tinker. "And you, too, if you will honor me?" His eyes studied Lando's tremendous physique. "You're a Sackett, I take it?"

"Orlando. And this here is the Tinker. He was a pack-peddler and tinker back in the hills."

"Oh, yes, I have heard of you, Tinker." Parmalee indicated the bottle. "Help yourself." And then he added, "You're the tinker who makes the knives...the Tinker-made knives that are the finest anywhere."

"We'd better move," Lando said. "Tyrel and them, they left at daybreak."

"Of course. Bartender, the bill please. Also," he said, speaking to O'Leary, "you might pass the word. I am now a full partner, and no gun wages will be paid to anyone."

Nolan emptied his glass. "When that word gets about," he said, "that Allen is goin' to be a mighty lonesome man."

Nolan, Lando, and Parmalee Sackett walked to the door, followed by the Tinker.

When the door had closed behind them, O'Leary turned to a couple of the loafers that were still in the room. "You boys cart those bodies to the stable, and I'll buy the drinks."

When they had gone out, Briscoe got up slowly from his chair and walked over to the bar. "I'll buy one," he said.

"Forget it. This one's on the house."

Briscoe picked up the glass and looked across the bar at the Irishman. "You think I was scared, don't you?"

O'Leary shrugged.

"You want to know something, Bob?" Briscoe said. "I *was* scared. I was scared plumb to death...and I never thought I'd admit that to anybody."

"He gave you good advice. You leave those guns off, and you ride out of here."

Briscoe nodded. He tried his drink, put the glass down, and took off his guns and placed them, rolled in their belts, on the bar. "You keep those," he said. "I never want to feel like that again...not never."

When he had left, O'Leary took the gun belts and the guns and hung them on a hook back of the bar.

After a few minutes, while rinsing a glass, he looked at them. He could remember the day when he had done the same thing. That was twenty years ago. "And I'm still alive," he said to himself.

The saloon was empty when the door opened and the girl walked in.

"I am Lorna," she said.

"Sorry. We don't serve ladies."

"Oh, come off it! I'm no lady, and you're going to serve me." She put both hands on the bar and looked straight at Bob O'Leary. "Have they caught him yet?"

"No."

"I hope they don't. I hope they never do."

Far down the trail toward the Mogollon country four riders were making dust.

FIFTEEN

They called it Wild Rye, and when opportunity offered, it lived up to the name. Ogletree, who owned what passed for a general store and saloon, had first seen the spot when he was a packer with General Crook in the expedition of 1872-73. He returned, put up a crude one-roomed, low-ceilinged log cabin, and went into business with seventy dollars' worth of stock.

Passers-by were few. Occasional Mormons from the settlement at Pine came down looking for drifted cattle or stolen horses, and once in a while there were prospectors or outlaws. Always, of course, there were Indians.

Ogletree was a tough man and a patient one, and he got along well with the Apaches. Usually they traded him fresh meat or skins, but from time to time there was a nugget. He had come into the Tonto prepared to live out his days there. But in less than two years he was setting out to find the source of the Apache gold, for he had learned there was a hidden valley somewhere in the Four Peaks region, only a few miles from his cabin, so one morning he rode away with a pack horse and following a hunch. Several weeks later the horse returned minus the pack and without Ogletree, nor was anything seen of them again.

But at the present time he was finishing his first year in the Tonto, and when the Lazy A riders came into the country Wild Rye had a population of five, including a squaw. From time to time some of the men hunting Tell Sackett stopped by for tobacco, remaining for a drink, and there had been talk.

Ogletree was a bald, stoop-shouldered man, usually seen in undershirt, suspenders, and pants, and carrying a rifle. He

115

was standing in the doorway smoking his pipe when he saw the two riders come up the creek. Both were tall, lean, and young. Each carried a rifle, each wore a gun. Their clothes were shabby, their hair uncut. When they had dismounted they walked up to his store, still carrying their rifles. They appraised him out of cold gray-green eyes and told him they wanted to eat.

"Drink?" he suggested.

"Eat," the taller one replied. And then he added, "I'm Flagan Sackett. This here's Galloway."

Ogletree led the way back into the low room, which was a step down from the level of the ground outside. As he dished up stew for them, he asked, "You any kin to Tell Sackett?"

"I reckon."

"They're huntin' him."

The two men made no response to this, and they ate without comment. When they had finished, Flagan laid two quarters on the counter.

"You tell those fellers they can stop huntin'. We come up to he'p him."

"There's been shootin' over on the East Fork...northwest of here, maybe fourteen, fifteen mile."

"Come on, Galloway. That's where we're goin'."

Only a few minutes had passed when Van Allen rode up to the store, accompanied by Sonora Macon and Rafe Romero, and two others whom Ogletree did not know. The storekeeper had seen Allen only once before, shortly after he himself arrived in Tonto. He would not have known him as the same man.

Vancouter Allen was forty years old, a big, strongly built man with thick arms and hands, good-looking in a hard, rough way. There was a tightness around his mouth and eyes that Ogletree had noticed before and had not liked, but now the lines there were sharply defined. Allen's cheeks were gaunt, his eyes hollow.

He carried himself with that impatient arrogance toward others that is often possessed by men who have succeeded by their own efforts, and too easily. A ruthless man, Allen had carried all before him, and had come to believe himself right in whatever he did, simply because he had always been successful. Yet he showed now that he was a frightened man. His own arrogance and an innate brutality had trapped him in the ugliest of situations, and he had been driven wild by fear of discovery. Through a crazy obsession, he found himself faced with ruin, and almost certain death.

He had been striding, hard-heeled, down the boardwalk in Globe when he saw Ange Sackett. He stopped so suddenly he almost staggered, but he recovered himself and walked on slowly. She was sitting quietly on the seat of a covered wagon that was loaded heavily with supplies. At the end of the walk he had turned to watch, and had seen Tell Sackett come out and mount the seat.

He had no idea who they were, and cared less. To him they were "movers," and so to be despised, but Ange was a beautiful girl, and the instant he saw her he wanted her. He had seen no such woman in years, nor any young white woman at all since leaving Texas, almost three months before. He was determined to have her, and never once suspected that he might be unsuccessful. The idea that a mover's woman would refuse him, a rich cattleman, was simply not to be considered.

So he had followed. He had said nothing to anyone, least of all to Swandle. He did make some casual comments about the movers, and so learned they were headed for the Mogollons, where he himself was going.

After leaving his outfit to prospect for the best grass and water, so he said, he followed the trail of the wagon. He saw Tell ride away, and was close enough to hear that he planned to scout around, and that he would be gone for several hours.

He had approached the wagon and had introduced himself, somewhat ostentatiously, as the owner of the Lazy A. When Ange seemed unimpressed, he had mentioned the number of cattle he had, and suggested that as they were neighbors they had better get along together. There was nothing subtle about his approach, and Ange was no fool. She had simply replied that it was a big country and there was small chance they would be neighbors. When he stepped from the saddle and came over to the wagon seat, she had ordered him off.

Vancouter Allen simply didn't believe she meant it. She was playing him along, he was sure, but he was not the sort of man to stand for that. He grabbed her and she slapped him, hard, across the mouth. The mules, startled, surged ahead a few steps and, caught off balance, Ange and Allen fell to the ground together.

Breaking free, Ange scrambled to her feet and ran. He caught up with her within a few steps and took hold of her. This time she had turned and raked him across the face with her nails. Something seemed to burst inside him, and when next he realized what he was doing, Ange Sackett lay on the ground, her clothing ripped and torn, her throat crushed, the skin broken under his powerful hands.

As suddenly as that, she was dead.

He got to his feet, bathed in cold sweat and horror.

There was no remorse in him. There was only fear. He had murdered a white woman...murdered the wife of a man who would soon be returning.

It had happened before, but then it was a squaw, and nobody cared about a squaw, at least nobody who was able to do anything about it. Of course, that time he had gotten away from there fast and nobody had ever connected it with him. Once or twice he had imagined that Swandle might have been suspicious, but he had said nothing. Whatever he might have suspected, Swandle kept to himself.

But this was different. This was a white woman.

Panic clutched at his throat. He forced himself to stand still, forced himself not to run. His hands would be coming soon, and they must find neither him nor the wagon.

The solution occurred to him suddenly. Several days

before, a rifle bullet had struck near him as he stood near the chuck wagon. It was probably a spent bullet from some hunter higher up in the woods, but now he could use that incident to his advantage. He mounted his horse, after hastily concealing the body, and raced to meet his oncoming riders. Rushing up to them, he told them he had been fired on, and described Sackett and the horse he rode.

"Find him and kill him!" he ordered. "I want him dead, do you hear? *Dead!*"

Only he was not dead, and he had lived to tell his story in Globe. And not long after that most of the old Lazy A crowd left Allen's outfit.

He had told the gunmen he hired that the rumors were all a pack of lies, but he knew safety lay only in the death of the girl's husband. He did not know the man's name and cared less. To Allen he was still simply a "mover" and of no consequence, one of the little men squatting on land that belonged by the right of rifle possession to the big outfits.

Once the man was dead, Allen felt that he could quiet the story. But when that failed to happen immediately, he had hired Lorna. She was young, unknown west of El Paso, and perfectly willing to earn two hundred dollars by spending the night beside a fire with a stranger and then screaming for help. Allen assured her it was simply a joke. She was not altogether sure of that, but she was sure that two hundred dollars was more money than she had had at one time for three years. Moreover, it was enough to take her to San Francisco and set her up in style.

Now, Allen was thinking, the end of the trail was near. His men had Sackett in a pocket from which he simply could not escape, and Vancouter Allen's fear had turned into a frightful, unreasoning hatred. He wanted to be in at the death.

In front of the store he dismounted stiffly, and walked over to the entrance. He paused there to look around once more. There was little enough to see.

Wild Rye at the time consisted of Ogletree's store, one smaller log cabin, a dugout, and across Rye Creek, two Indian wickiups. There was a pole corral with a water trough, and some distance off a shed where Ogletree made his whiskey.

Inside the store things didn't look much better. There was a counter with a row of shelves behind it, a table, three chairs and a box, and an unmade bed. On the shelves were several empty bottles, a half-dozen gallon cans, some boxes of shells, and assorted odds and ends of cheap gimcracks of the sort that might interest an Indian. There was also a short-legged bench on which stood a barrel with a spigot. At one side of the room was a fireplace.

"What have you got to eat?" Allen demanded.

Ogletree continued washing the dishes left by the two Sacketts for a full minute before he replied. "Stew."

"Any good?" Allen asked. "I mean, is it fit to eat."

"Those two fellers who just left didn't complain. They ate it right up."

"Some of my men?"

Ogletree turned and looked at Allen with ill-concealed relish. "They said they was huntin' your men. Their name was Sackett."

Allen's head came around sharply. Sonora Macon, just inside the door, had also heard. "Young? Were they young fellers?"

"One maybe eighteen or so...the other a year or so older. I'm just guessing, of course. But they're young."

"The same two that killed Dodie, Ryland, and Collins," Macon said. "Let's go get them, boss."

"Wait," Allen said. "They'll keep. I'm hungry."

"They won't run," Ogletree commented, "not them two."

"Nobody asked you," Allen said shortly. "All right, let's have that stew."

He had finished eating and had lighted a cigar when Dancer rode up. Dancer had quit. He had quit the Lazy A and was glad of it, but he could not wait to tell the news he had. He strode into the saloon and ordered a cup of coffee.

He turned to look at Vancouter Allen. "You got you a new partner," he said.

"What's that?"

Dancer shrugged. "First thing he done was fire all those boys you hired. I mean all that were back at the camp. Said he wouldn't pay a dime of fighting wages to anyone."

He had their attention, every bit of it.

"What are you talking about?" Allen demanded, his voice rising.

"Swandle sold out. He got his price and he sold out. By this time he's halfway to Prescott."

"I don't believe it," Allen said contemptuously. "He wouldn't have the guts to sell, and who would he find to buy?"

"Man came to him." Dancer wanted to prolong it, but couldn't wait to see what Allen's expression would be. "Man name of Parmalee Sackett."

Allen sat very still. He could hear his heart pounding with heavy beats. His big hands rested on the table before him and his confused brain tried to absorb the information.

Swandle had sold out...sold out. He had a new partner. A partner named Parmalee Sackett. And Sackett had fired his men.

"Are you making this up? By the Lord Harry, Dancer, if you—"

"I ain't makin' it up," Dancer said innocently. "It was right after Al Zabrisky got killed."

Allen stared down at the bowl of stew. It had smelled wonderful, but suddenly his appetite was gone. He no longer wanted to ask questions, he feared the answers too much. Of course, Al had been killed by a Sackett.

This time it was no use to wait, and Dancer knew it. He leaned his elbow on the bar and looked at his drink. "*Nolan* Sackett done it. You know...that Nevada, California outlaw. He's one of them, too, it seems. He's headed this way with that there Parmalee Sackett, and Lando Sackett, and a feller they call the Tinker.

"They're comin' from all over the country, Allen, an' if you'll take my advice you'll hit the saddle and light a shuck out of here. I don't think you'd get away, but you can try. Those feudin', fightin' mountain boys, they surely stick together."

"*Shut up!*"

Nobody said anything. Ogletree took a bottle from under the counter and filled Dancer's glass, waving away the cowboy's protest. "On the house," he said.

Vancouter Allen shoved his chair back, got to his feet, and walked out of the door. The gunmen followed him. Outside, Sonora Macon spoke quietly. "Boss? About that partner, now? Can he really stop our wages?"

"I'm paying you!" Allen said sharply. "I don't need him. I've got the money right here!" He slapped his belt.

Macon exchanged a glance with Romero, who shrugged. "Sure," Macon said. "All right, boss."

Inside the store somebody suddenly began to sing "The Hunters of Kentucky." Ogletree chimed in on the chorus.

Allen, his features ugly with anger, rode away to the north, up Rye Creek.

There was nothing to worry about, he told himself. Tell Sackett was no more than fourteen or fifteen miles away, treed up against the mesa where he could not escape.

They would be there by nightfall.

SIXTEEN

So here at last was I, William Tell Sackett, and a far piece I'd come from the Cumberlands, a far piece...to die with my back to the wall in the Mogollons.

It left me with no good thought to know I had come so far and done so little with my life. I'd fought for my country in the War Between the States, to save the Union, and I would do it again. I'd fought the redskins, too, and driven cattle north from Texas to Montana, and helped to open up some of the most lovely land under heaven.

At the end, it all came to nothing. Ange murdered, and my death nearing me at the hands of the same man, and no son to leave behind.

Most of all, I hated to leave Allen alive, he who had killed my lovely girl. There's some, I'm told, who frown upon revenge, and perhaps it is better so, but I was a mountain boy, reared in a feudal land, living my life through by the feudal code, and our law was the Mosaic law of an eye for an eye.

They were waiting now, waiting for somebody to come before they moved in for the kill. That somebody had to be Van Allen. He wanted to be here, to be sure I was actually dead. He wanted to look into my dead eyes and know that he was safe. There would be talk, of course, but nobody would push such talk very far in the face of the guns Allen could command. Especially when the only man who could give Allen the lie was dead and buried.

They were waiting for him, then, and that meant that somehow I must stay alive until he got here. I must stay alive and save a bullet for him. Somehow, even in being destroyed, I must destroy him.

I looked about, seeking out a hole into which I might

crawl, anywhere to hide. There was no place to run, nor had I the strength for it. It was root hog or die right here. But the place offered me little.

The cliff reared up red and steep behind me, and along the lower reaches it was scattered over with scrub cedar. It was broken, eroded rock, with much stuff fallen from above. The canyons opening to right and left were steep, places where a man might crawl if he could find the cover for it.

Where I was, lay a sort of trough that ran for several yards. Larger slabs of fallen rock had landed out a few feet from the base, and cedar or yucca had grown up among the slabs, so that I could not be seen, even if I moved.

There's seldom a corner so tough a man might not find a way out, if he has the nerve and the strength to try. Nerve enough I had, but I was played out, worn to a frazzle by the exhaustion of weeks of running, piled onto the wounds I'd had.

When I looked down at myself, showing through my torn shirt the way I was, it was a shocking sight. I was a strong-muscled man, but lean. Only now every rib showed. I was ga'nted up like a share-cropper's mule, just a rack of bones and hide.

For a time I lay there watching them. Though I thought they must know where I was, they were avoiding this place, searching out the rocks down below just to make sure I hadn't fooled them, and it was that that gave me the idea.

My strength was slight enough, and going up, if I found a way, would give me nothing but the chance to die on higher ground. So what if, after they'd searched well over the lower ground, I slipped down there and let them move on up, to search up here?

If I could get below, then I'd have them, or some of them, against the hill where they figured to have me. And when Van Allen came, he would be down there, close to me.

Lying quiet, I studied the terrain below, and saw a way it might be done.

There was a sight of Injun in me, though it came of

learning and thinking, and not of blood. I'd run the hills with the Cherokees as a boy, them as were called the Overhill Cherokees because they lived west of the mountains. So I laid Injun eyes on the land below me, and saw a slight chance in the way I might go. It was the only chance I had.

They'd not be expecting me to come toward them now. They would watch the likely places, and the one I'd chosen wasn't that...it offered little enough place for a man to hide. But the thing I knew was that the best place to hide was in the mind of the searcher, for all men have blind spots in the mind. They rarely see what they do not expect to see, and their minds hold a blindness to what seems unreasonable. Nobody but an Apache would think to choose the way I'd chosen. And if any Apaches were down there, they would not be expecting Apache thinking of a white man.

There was open ground to my left, and it was there I went, edging along, for I had to go slow, and needed to for the quietness my going called for.

There were no big boulders here, no gullies or cracks, and no brush at all. There was just rugged desert ground with a few places here and there, only inches deep, and scattered rocks no bigger than your head. Tufts of bunch grass grew among the yucca, but nothing larger.

First I rubbed my rifle barrel all over with dust to take the shine from it. My clothes, so stained with dust and sweat, were almost of the ground's own color, mingled with bloodstains and the tears where my sun-browned skin showed through.

Flat on my belly I went. Inch by inch I wormed along, through a space where a few cedars grew. I came to a fairly shallow place and went into it, and there I lay still for a bit. Then on I went, working along, moving so slightly that it scarcely seemed like movement at all.

Apaches had done it...I'd known of a case where a man grazed his horse with it tied to a rope and the rope's end in his hand...and an Apache slipped up in the bright afternoon sunlight and cut the rope and eased off with the horse. He swung astride him and was gone, leaving the man holding the rope and looking foolish.

My mouth was dry as dust, dry from fear of being seen, and dry from having no drink in many hours. My heart pounded heavily and my head ached from the hunger and tiredness that was in me. But my rifle was in my hand, and when the moment came, if I could only find a rest for it, I'd take a good lot with me down the road to death.

A long, slow hour passed. Once a boot crunched within a few feet above me as I lay still. Another time I heard men talking of a fight there'd been, of men killed with violence, and guns flaring and thundering in O'Leary's place…and then I heard the name of Nolan Sackett.

Nolan! He had come, then. Nolan was an outlaw Sackett, a wild and desperate man, and one who had pulled me from a bad hole in California not too far back. Me they might kill, but now I could be sure they'd know the Sackett men before the summer was gone.

There was no doubt in me that I would die, for there was no way out that I could see. For minutes, long minutes, I lay perfectly still, right in the open with those hunting men about me, knowing my only safety lay in their searching minds, for it was up on the higher ground they looked now, and not right there below them.

Suddenly I heard the beat of hoofs on the trail. Riders coming! Then a harsh voice sounded and something within me jolted and my heart seemed to miss a beat, and within me a terrible hatred came up, for I knew that must be the voice.

"We've got him, Mr. Allen," somebody was answering. "He's right up there in those rocks. We've got men along the rim above him, and there's not a chance he can get away."

"All right. Go get him." That voice again…how far from me?

They started at once…there must have been a dozen men down there, as well as those on the cliffs above. I heard them start, and I reached back and slipped the thong from my six-shooter.

"Put lead on that rock behind him," somebody said. "That will flush him out!"

A half-dozen Winchesters began feeding lead against the hillside, trying to do what the Army had done to the Apaches in the Salt River cave, not more than a whistle and a yell from here. Glancing bullets whined and whipped through the air, and had I been back there I'd have been a lucky man to escape death.

"He's dead, or gone," a man called out. "There's no sign of him."

Ahead of me I heard voices. "No, stay here," Allen was saying. "We've got a better view of the mountain from here. If he escapes them, we've got him."

"Boss," another voice spoke up quickly, "there's some-body coming down the trail!"

"Some of the boys, Macon. I told them all to close in."

"They don't look familiar." Macon's voice was doubting.

"I can see our boys up on the hill above him." This voice had a Spanish accent, ever so slight...would that be Romero, the Mexican gunfighter? "Which one wears a black coat?"

.   I lay perfectly still, but my mind felt queer. Somehow I couldn't bring my thoughts to focus, and there was a terrible weakness upon me. I daren't move my head, for I felt sure I was within view of them all, and any movement would be seen. Yet it was now or never.

My left hand pushed the rifle forward, holding it clear of the rocks to make no sound. I turned my head so I could look straight ahead, and I saw a clump of bear grass there, and to my left another.

Suddenly a shout went up behind me. "He's *gone!* Damn it, *he's gone!*"

And then another voice called down, and it was a voice I knew.

"All of you down there...back up and drop your guns or we'll cut you to doll rags!"

That was Orrin...*Orrin here?*

Allen was standing in his stirrups...for the first time I

saw my enemy. "What the hell?" he called. "Who's *that?*"

Now I had it to do, so I came up off the ground, rifle in my left hand, my right waiting for the feel of my Colt.

Out of the corner of my eye I could see a row of men along that hill where I'd been lying, just above there where the bullets had gone. They were all moving slowly down the slope.

Orrin was there, all right, and Tyrel. And there were some others that I did not know.

The three men in front of me were staring up the hill. I was somewhat to their left. Close to where I had stood up, there was an ocotillo with its many spines in a stiff clump, flaring out from its base, and just beyond that a yucca. I had stood up so soundlessly that it was a moment before they saw me.

The riders on the road were drawing close. Then I heard Nolan Sackett's voice. "You boys wanted a fight, now you got it."

Sonora Macon, Rafe Romero, and Van Allen...all three were looking at me. I lowered the butt of my Winchester to the ground to steady myself. I doubted if I could hold the rifle steady enough without a rest, but I wasn't worried about a six-shooter. I could shoot one of those if I could still breathe.

Allen had been standing in his stirrups, now he lowered himself gently into the saddle. I thought he looked a little gray under the dark stubble of his beard.

"You been huntin' me, Allen. And I been huntin' you."

He looked at me, staring hard. I do not know if he wanted to see the look of the man he'd wronged and tried to kill, or if he was only looking at a man he expected to kill, but I knew deep down within me that no matter what came to me, Van Allen was staring down the black muzzle of death.

"Who are those men?" he demanded.

"Sacketts, mostly," I said. "They're of the Sackett family of Tennessee, or those who stand close to them. I don't know all of them myself."

Cap Rountree was there, and a strange-looking man with

gold rings in his ears, the like of which I never did see, but I was a mountain man and had heard tell of the Tinker.

Suddenly a tall man with iron gray at his temples and a coat with a handsome cut was standing beside me. He was a Sackett, all right, although one I'd never seen. "I'm Falcon Sackett, Tell. My son is here also."

"There's going to be shootin'," I said.

"I'll stand with you, William Tell, and a better man I never stood beside."

Overhead the sun was hot, somewhere a horse blew dust from his nostrils and stomped his feet. Allen's gunmen were holding ready for the word, only Allen wasn't giving it. He was looking at me.

Maybe it was the heat waves dancing, maybe it was a blur in my vision. Everything seemed vague and whirly there before me, kind of shimmering, with the shadows of men beyond it.

"She never had much, Mr. Allen," I said. "I'll never forget the first time we met, high up in the Colorado mountains. She said, 'I'm Ange Kerry, and I'm most glad you found me.' It was a heart-tearing thing, the way she spoke, and the littleness and loneliness of her.

"I hoped to make it up to her. I hoped to bring her happiness in this fine new land where the pines stood tall and the water ran cold over the rocks. I wanted to build her a house of her own, and fix it proper, and we'd have our children there. That's what I wanted, Mr. Allen, and you murdered her. You found her alone and you broke the flesh of her throat in your hands. You took the life out of her, Mr. Allen."

Macon shifted his feet. "I didn't know he done that."

"He did it."

"I didn't mean to. I thought...well, I figured she was some mover's woman."

"No matter...she was a woman. As for movers, you're a mover yourself, Mr. Allen. Where did you move from? And why? Is there blood behind you?"

My knees felt funny and I didn't quite know what I was saying. I could see him up there on his horse, peering at me.

"By God," he shouted suddenly, "I paid you to kill him. Now *kill him!*"

Some fool must have moved...and all at once the day was thundering guns and the wicked stab of flame. I could feel my own gun bucking in my grip, and I was stumbling forward toward that man on the horse. I saw his gun up and firing, saw his face twisted in an awful wrench of agony, and saw blood start from his chest. My next bullet ripped the side of his face away, and he fell down, but he came up and threw both hands in front of his face and began to scream. I shot through his hands until my gun was empty, and I was down on my knees and no longer wanted to shoot anybody or anything.

Orrin had me by the shoulders. "Easy, man! Easy, now. It's all over."

When I shook off his hands and staggered up, I saw Macon was down and Romero had fallen off to one side. All around men were standing with their hands up, and nobody wanted to fight any more.

Tyrel walked over to me. It was the first time I had seen him wearing a gun. "Are you all right, Tell?"

Me, I nodded.

"Let's go home," he said.

Behind me I heard Parmalee saying, "Flagan, you and Galloway would please me if you'd stay and help me round up these cattle."

We stopped in Globe and the lot of us lined up in O'Leary's place, all of us together, more Sacketts than I'd ever seen before...or anybody else, I guess.

Me, standing there amongst them, I looked around and I knew I was not alone, and I'd never be alone again.